Blind Date, Checkmate

Excerpt

"I never stopped loving you," he said as we both got to the door.

Liar. I whirled around and glared. "I was seventeen and it's been nine years. We've both grown up. I'm not the same stupid kid and I won't be so gullible this time." Why did he keep drawing me into these conversations? "So far, Logan, you're all talk and no action. The story of your life. No follow-through." I tried to get past him but he blocked the door. I backed up when I noticed his eyes ablaze, thinking maybe I'd pushed him too far.

As if I were his prey, he caged me against the wall with his arms. I pressed my back into cold wall so I wouldn't feel his thighs brushing mine. He only moved closer, a breath away, the friction of our bodies sending an inferno through me.

Oh, yes, that had definitely been missing in my life.

"You want me to follow through, I'm ready right now," he growled softly.

Me too. But Logan was the last guy I'd go there with. Although it wouldn't exactly be a hardship re-enacting certain moments with someone that stunning, deep down I was still bruised by his past rejection.

But I couldn't deny I was tempted.

I'd never had a relationship that lasted. If I was doomed to a life of loneliness, it almost seemed justifiable to take happiness where I could find it, even if only temporarily.

Logan inched toward me, his lips at my temple. My pulse spiked as he sucked my earlobe between his lips and I shuddered.

"I knew you still loved me," he whispered in my ear.

His words slapped me back to reality. A temporary fling with him would only bring me a lifetime of more pain. No. Way. "Oh, honey, you're confusing love with lust." I patted his cheek a little harder than necessary and pushed on his chest. "A guy like you should know better. Let's go eat. I'm hungry." I sailed past him knowing I'd thrown him a nice curve.

I'd just taken his bishop. Score one point for me.

THROWN TO THE WOLVES
SHAPES OF AUTUMN:
THE LEGEND OF HANNAH + ELI

VERONICA
BLADE

Blind Date, Checkmate

VERONICA BLADE

PUBLISHING

Gardnerville, Nevada

Crush Publishing, Inc
Gardnerville, NV
www.CrushPublishing.com

ISBN 978-0-9798869-9-7

Cover design by Rose Nomura

For my wonderful husband

Chapter One

Various ways to murder my best friend flashed through my mind. But if I got rid of her, she wouldn't be around for me to talk to. Then I'd just be even more lonely. Despite the guys I'd dated, they'd rarely tempted me enough to get me into the bedroom. I was used to living without a soul mate. I didn't want to live without my best friend too.

There were other ways to punish her for secretly arranging a blind date for me — and waiting until practically the last minute to tell me. Ways that would drag out the pain, make her suffer longer. I'd spent two hours every day for the past nine years working off my sexual tension at the gym. I could take her.

"I'm not going, Ginny." I shot up from the sofa, my hands slamming to my hips. "Call him and cancel. Besides, you're forgetting Jared. Going out with another guy doesn't seem right."

Granted, shortly after our first and only date, Jared had moved a hundred miles away. I considered that a fairly easy weekend commute. And our date had gone well, as far as I could tell. Although he still seemed interested in me, and he was easy on the eyes, I wasn't sure how I felt about him. I needed to spend more time with him to see. Who knew what I'd get with this last minute blind date?

Ginny's eyes snapped to mine as she, too, rose from the couch to go toe-to-toe with me. "Nothing against Jared. I like him, Shelby. I've known him longer than you have. But he did leave. If you'd made it to a third date, that'd be a different story. In the meantime, you can date another guy."

"Maybe I don't want to date another guy." My lip jutted out. "It might work out with Jared."

"Or it might not. You should keep your options open." Ginny canted her head and gave me a sly smile. "But you'll never know unless you meet this guy."

"But a blind date, Ginny?" I grimaced, then shook my head. "No. I'm not that desperate." Not yet, anyway.

She rolled her eyes. "Fine. I give up. If you want to cancel, you'll have to do it yourself. Here's his number." She reached into her jeans pocket, pulled out a tiny piece of paper and thrust it at me.

"What? No way." I shook my head violently. "You're the one who set it up—"

She sighed and stuck the paper back in her pocket. "As usual, I was looking out for you. If you think I'm going to be the bad guy here, you can forget it."

Bad guy? Guilt swept through me and I hesitated, but then I saw her lips quirk.

I narrowed my eyes. She thought she was so slick.

I was slicker. I shrugged, putting on an air of indifference. "Then the poor guy's going to sit at the restaurant and wait for a date that never shows."

"Trust me, a guy that hot won't be alone for long. But if you blow him off, don't be complaining to me about your love life — or lack thereof."

Apparently, I wasn't as slick as I thought because the words 'a guy that hot' piqued my interest. How hot were we talking? Better looking than Jared? That would be saying something.

I reconsidered. Whether it was Ginny or I who called and cancelled, some guy was going to have his plans for the evening ruined. What if he had a fragile ego? Unlikely if he was gorgeous, but possible.

Jared and I had no plans to get together anytime soon so I didn't have anything better to do for a while, other than work.

Let's not forget Ginny thought this guy was hot. If nothing else, I'd get a nice meal out of the date.

A girl has to eat.

"Fine." I rolled my eyes to keep up the pretense. Ginny would gloat if she thought she'd won and I wouldn't want her to make a habit of setting me up on blind dates. "When and where?"

She smiled smugly. "You're meeting him at six tonight at The Boat House. Remember where it is?" She grabbed her purse from my overstuffed chair.

"Yeah, I sell real estate, remember? I can find anything in Sacramento." I rose and followed her to my front door. "So what's this guy's name?"

"Have fun." She flashed a mischievous grin. "And let me know how it goes," she threw over her shoulder, just before disappearing outside.

"Hey, wait a second—" Too late. She was gone. Great. I checked my watch. Two hours to kill. Grabbing my phone, I texted Ginny.

What's Hot Guy's name?

I stared at my phone but it didn't ring or buzz or anything else. I plopped onto my black suede sofa and flipped on the giant flat screen TV. A second later, I turned it off and glanced around my living room. I had everything a girl could want: a nice house, great friends and a profession I loved — and was damn good at it. But that wasn't enough. Loneliness swept through me. Unfortunately, it was an all-too-familiar feeling. One I'd lived with for years.

All because of one man.

Chances were that even if I liked my date tonight and he liked me, even if we went out and kept going out and, even if it led to sex, I'd still be lonely. Because let's face it, whoever I dated would never be the man I really wanted.

Logan Starks.

Nope, no one could measure up to good old Logan. The love of my life. The boy who'd taken my virginity nine years ago at age seventeen. The dog who'd moved to Los Angeles to live with his dad, then dumped me after stringing me along for months.

Even now, a familiar pain sliced through me. No wonder Ginny had blindsided me with a blind date. She probably knew better than anyone that a part of me was still hung up on Logan. A big part. But I refused to give him any more of my mental energy. At least not tonight. He didn't deserve it.

My attention turned to the stack of mail by the front door. I deserted the couch to sort through the pile. At the bottom, Logan's face smiled up at me from the cover of the latest Movers and Shakers magazine. I bit my lip and told myself to toss the rag in the trash. In the end, I couldn't.

Enslaved by my curiosity, I took the magazine to the sofa with me and flipped through the pages to find his interview. They had given him a whole spread, complete with multiple photos — Logan at the tender age of twenty-three when his debut novel had hit the New York Times bestseller list, Logan at his first movie premier wearing a tux and a blond starlet on his arm, a quote from a reviewer praising the work of the great writer and another announcing his new three-book deal and hefty advance.

Page after page recorded his epic moments in the last four years, but I already knew about most of them. You didn't have to leave your house to hear about Logan Starks.

The gossip magazines and tabloids didn't normally pursue novelists. Even the biggest names in books rarely made their way into those coveted pages. But the paparazzi loved Logan's face — along with most of America's female population. Being spotted at posh clubs in Beverly Hills with the co-star of his first movie had spiraled him into the limelight and given him a secure spot on the A-list. He'd become a household name and forgotten all about me.

I gave myself another mental slap for caring. Hollywood could have Logan. I didn't need him. Besides, who knew where things would lead with Jared? Or this blind date? I had options. And if I worked fewer hours and made myself more available for dates, I'd probably have even more options.

My pep talk worked and my shoulder muscles stopped cramping.

After tossing the magazine in the trash, I opened the fridge, took out several containers of leftovers and dumped them on the image of Logan's perfect face. "Bubbye."

I checked my watch. Five-fifteen. I only had about thirty minutes to get ready. No way would I go on a blind date and not look my best. That meant I'd be slightly late. The question was whether to dress sexy or classy. Why couldn't I be both?

Standing in front of my open closet, I grabbed a black pencil skirt just a hair too short for showing houses and a soft pink cashmere tank top that clung to my every curve. After choosing a pair of too-high strappy heels that brought me to nearly five eleven, I laid everything on the bed.

At record speed, I showered and straightened my long auburn waves. I skimped on the make-up since I didn't want my date to think I was trying too hard.

Or that I needed to. Men responded better when they believed you don't care.

I checked my watch again. I'd be even later than I thought. Crap. Had to hurry.

Wait. How would I find him? Ginny still hadn't returned my text. Talk about the blind leading the Blind Date. My heels clicked as I strutted to the front door and texted her again.

What does Mr. Hottie look like? Any identifying marks?

I imagined Mr. Hottie having a tattoo or two, maybe something on his stomach that led to his happy trail.

Unfortunately, in my mind, Mr. Hottie looked a whole lot like Logan.

◆ ◆ ◆

I stood outside the entrance of The Boat House with sweaty palms. I was ten minutes late, but I couldn't bring myself to go inside. Why was I nervous? Not like I'd never been on a date before. Somehow, this one was different. And this was more than just a blind date. Something about the way Ginny had set it up without asking, how she wouldn't call it off, filled me with suspicion. She really wanted me to go out with this guy, but why?

It didn't matter. He still wasn't going to be Logan. He could never be. After all, Logan and I had a pretty long history.

Our moms had been best friends so he and I had grown up together. He was a year older than me, fifteen, when he asked me to be his girlfriend. We were together nearly three years and I never once imagined I'd be with anyone but him for the rest of my life.

A couple months before my seventeenth birthday, Logan arrived at my house, face flushed and hands trembling. His parents were getting a divorce and his dad was moving to Los Angeles. They'd agreed that Logan would go with his dad and his sister would stay with his mom. He wasn't given a choice.

We'd intended to make the long distance thing work. He kept promising that when he turned eighteen, he'd come back. He never did. Eventually, he stopped returning my emails or calls.

And it was over. I'd lost the love of my life and my best friend.

No matter who I dated afterwards, I'd always remember what I'd felt like when I was with Logan. I wanted another love like that. If I couldn't have something that great, why bother?

I'd probably die of old age, still single and childless. I was so screwed.

But I was already at the restaurant and my stomach growled. I told myself to go inside and meet Mr. Hot and Gorgeous. I snorted, beginning to suspect Ginny was exaggerating the physical appeal of my Blind Date when she replied to my text with, You'll know him when you see him. Look for the most gorgeous guy there.

I'd barely stopped myself from shooting back a text: If he's so hot, how come you're not going out with him? She'd only remind me of her husband. Sure, rub my face in it.

A couple exited the restaurant holding hands and laughing, eyes shining as they gazed at each other. Love, the kind that brought loyalty, trust and security. The kind that meant if you got in a huge fight, he'd still be there in the morning. The kind of love where the guy didn't dump you and stomp on your heart. My chest tightened over old memories and I took a deep breath. Time to go in and meet my date.

Inside, I forced a polite smile at the hostess. "I'm meeting someone. I'll just have a look around." Walking the aisle, I scanned the tables for anyone sitting alone. Men glanced at me when I passed by and I recognized their looks. Appreciation. Admiration. Lust. And that familiar feeling filled me. Power.

Too bad I couldn't harness the power long enough to make a man fall in love and stay there forever. At least, not one that I wanted.

I spotted a guy wearing a dark blue sweater and jeans with a leather jacket hung over the back of his chair. Even from his back, he looked like he could be the best looking guy in the room. Dark wavy hair, broad shoulders. A quick survey of the restaurant also told me he was the only one in the entire place without a tablemate.

My stomach fluttered.

Time to see if he and I clicked. I came up around him on his right and he twisted away from me, checking his jacket pocket for something. As he turned back, I caught his profile.

Oh. Dear. God.

With my feet rooted to the floor, seconds passed before I realized my mouth had dropped open.

That guy wasn't my date. Ginny wouldn't do that to me. This was just some joke. Whoever Ginny had set me up with had to be around here somewhere. I resumed walking and stumbled on my own toe. Regaining my balance, I held my head high and forged on. I passed the man, my legs moving like they were wading through sludge.

"Shelby?"

I halted, my fists rolling into a ball.

I could do this. I could see him again without falling apart. Stretching taller, more confident, I whirled to face him.

"So good to see you." He beamed and motioned me over to his table.

I stared at him, soaking in the features that I'd seen just an hour ago on the cover of a magazine. They were exactly as I remembered. Same steel gray eyes, which had gazed at me like I were an angel. Same dark hair I'd run my fingers through. Same hands that had cupped my face as his lips had whispered how much he loved me.

But that had been a lifetime ago.

My jaw tightened but I forced myself to speak. "Hello, Logan."

Chapter Two

"What are you doing here?" I asked.

Logan's brows furrowed. "Didn't Ginny tell you?"

I flinched at the confirmation of Ginny's betrayal. Why had she done it? She knew how devastated I had been when Logan had turned cold. I couldn't imagine what she'd hoped to accomplish by this fake date. Unless she was under the impression I still loved him and that he had feelings for me?

Dizziness made me blink. My heart thudded.

A waitress barreled down the aisle carrying a tray of drinks and I squeezed closer to Logan's table to make room. Logan's table. Not mine. I wasn't staying. Whatever the reason was for this set-up, it wasn't because he had feelings for me. Not after all this time.

"Shelby—" He started to stand and I held up a hand as if to stop him.

He lowered back to his chair, waiting for me to speak.

But when I opened my mouth to tell him off, nothing came out. And when I tried to move my legs to walk away from him, they remained frozen.

He sighed. "If Ginny didn't tell you, this must be quite a shock. W-Why don't you sit down? Since you're already here." He waved toward the chair across from him.

I shivered at the gravelly tenor of his voice. Funny, I'd been observing him the last five years as he matured to a man. But the pictures had been a flat, dull version of him. Live and in person, his mannerisms and sexy voice brought his good looks to life.

I couldn't let his blinding beauty distract me. I was in survival mode.

"Why would I want to do that? I—" A waitress bumped into me, scowling as she maneuvered around me.

"Because you're in everyone's way," Logan teased. Any nervousness I may have imagined a moment ago seemed to have vanished, giving way to confidence and the full dazzling smile I'd seen in countless magazines. "Sit down, just for a minute."

I obeyed halfheartedly, but only because if I stood there much longer, someone was going to nail me with food or drink just to get me to move. Besides, people were staring. At him. Mr. Hollywood Sex God.

The hottest guy in the place. No kidding, Ginny.

Now that the shock of seeing him had worn off, confusion set in. Why had Ginny tricked me and what the hell did Logan want? I gripped my tiny purse in an effort to steady my fingers and hide my jitters. I could survive this. I'd be okay. Regardless why I'd been lured here, Logan could never know how much I still wanted him.

"Why am I on a blind date with you, Logan?" I asked in my most impersonal voice, the one I reserved for people I disliked. It felt rusty and foreign in my throat, since I rarely needed to use it.

A tall dark-haired woman with a seriously grim set to her mouth stopped at our table. "Hi, I'm Marcia. I'll be your server. Can I get you sonething to drink?" she asked me.

"No, thank—"

"She'll have one of these." He held up his wine glass. "Thank you."

Marcia turned to Logan and her eyes sparked with recognition. But she didn't crack a smile. "Coming right up." She pivoted and melted into the crowd.

I leaned back in the chair and folded my arms over my chest. "You're wasting your money. I'm not staying long enough to drink it."

"Then go thirsty, but I'm happy to waste more money. Are you hungry?" He casually lifted the menu and immersed himself in it as if he didn't care. Against my will, I relaxed enough for curiosity to once again raise its head. I wasn't sure if I was more irritated with Logan for reeling me in with his indifference or annoyed with myself for falling for it. Stubbornly, I refused to pick up my menu.

Logan glanced at me over his. "You can order whatever you want. The most expensive item on the menu, if you like. Just hear me out, Shelby. Ginny obviously thought what I had to say to you was important."

He sounded so serious, but he was right. Despite my initial feelings of betrayal, Ginny must have had a good reason for bringing me here. I couldn't imagine what that was.

"Fine. Dinner. Then I'm outta here." I perused my menu but I couldn't focus. All the letters registered in my head as scribbles.

"My sister and I ate here last year."

He'd visited last year? I suppose if I'd kept in touch with his sister Kristin, she would have told me Logan was around. But I hadn't. After our breakup, she'd reminded me of him and it had been too painful for me. After a while, the prospect of reconnecting with her had seemed too awkward. I missed her though.

"I had the steak and mushrooms sautéed in a wine sauce. Comes with steamed asparagus and mashed potatoes, if I remember correctly. Damn good."

Sounded like it could be and I still couldn't concentrate enough to read the menu. "I'll have that. Where's our waitress?"

On cue, Marcia arrived and set a glass in front of me without acknowledging my existence. But she eyed Logan, a sly smile waiting for him. Was her blouse undone one more button now or just my imagination?

"Are you ready to order?" she purred.

I rolled my eyes.

"Two of these." Logan pointed at the menu and smiled. It wasn't quite a flirty I'm-hot-and-I-know-it smile, but it was close. "Please."

Logan didn't speak after she left. He just looked at me and I felt myself wanting to lean toward him. To reacquaint myself with those full lips. I shook off the vision. Whipping out my cell phone, I began texting Ginny. She'd get a piece of my mind for her shenanigans.

"For you," Logan said.

My fingers froze on the keyboard and I shifted my focus to him. "What?"

"You asked me why I was here."

My brows flew up. "You're here for me?" To talk to me about something important, maybe. But to say he was here for me. No Way.

"Yeah." His gaze lowered to the white cloth napkin where his fingers folded and unfolded the linen. "I... I've been wanting to talk to you for a long time."

I slapped the cloth-covered table. "You've had nine years, buddy. Now all of a sudden you want to talk? Well, go ahead. Talk." I looked pointedly at my watch. "Clock is ticking. Once I eat, I'm leaving and we're not doing this again."

Logan inhaled deeply, then met my eyes. "I've missed you."

"Oh, please!" I returned to typing profanity into

Ginny's message even though I could barely see the keys through my shock. He'd missed me! My traitorous heart rejoiced.

Nine years, my brain shouted back.

"I deserve that. I don't blame you for not trusting me. But I'd like you to give me a chance. There's a reason I stopped calling you after I moved to LA."

I could barely hear him over the buzzing in my ears. He wanted a chance for what, to justify breaking my heart?

Nope. No second chances. Sure, I'd missed him. Compared him to every man I met. Tortured myself with reading Hollywood rags just so I'd have another glimpse at his gorgeous face. But I wasn't a complete fool. Whatever had brought him here couldn't be genuine feelings for me. Not after all this time. No, he obviously wanted something from me. That was it.

I looked up from my phone again. "Food comes slow here. I'd say you have about an hour to tell me what you really want. As for why you stopped calling me, that was ages ago. You did me favor. I could care less, really. And if you say another word about it, I'm leaving."

He stared at me, then raised both hands in surrender. "Okay. Fine. Clean slate, if that's what you want."

His quick acceptance to sweep it all under the rug ignited my fury and my limbs trembled. "We'll just gloss over it, like it never happened." Bitterness dripped from my words. "We'll forget how you promised me forever, then dumped me. And later, how you told me you didn't love me and that one day, I'd be grateful to be free of you. Well, guess what, Logan? It's 'one day' and you were right. I am glad you dumped me and I am grateful you didn't let me waste one more minute on someone who didn't love me. We're both better off now."

"I hurt you," he said softly. "I'm sorry."

Oh, no. He didn't get to play the big man taking responsibility for his actions. And he couldn't make me feel guilty for being angry. Even if he was sincere and wanted me back — and that last part was a stretch — whatever love he felt wouldn't last. Just like it didn't before.

The theory percolating in my mind was that he wanted closure, for some reason. Maybe he was engaged and wanted to address his past? I wasn't going to let him off that easy. "If it took nine years to say it, you can't be that sorry." I rose from my chair. "Ladies room."

Checking under the two stalls, I made sure the bathroom was empty. I leaned against the wall and sucked in a lungful of air. Instead of giving me a sense of calm, the quiet brought back memories of years ago. Of a happiness that could only exist by finding a soulmate. But the Logan I had known no longer existed and the man at the table was not my soulmate, no matter how much I wanted him to be. I should have left the restaurant as soon as I'd recognized him. He'd said he had something important to tell me, but all he'd fed me so far was a line about missing me.

The smart thing to do would be to walk out of the

restaurant and go home. To run away from him as fast as I could. It wasn't too late. But leaving now would show Logan he held some kind of power over me.

Of course, he did, even if it was just bad memories, but I couldn't let him know that.

Maybe Ginny had done me a favor after all. Tonight could be my chance to get closure. I'd face him head on, like the mature adult I'd become. Then I'd get on with my life, free of regrets forever.

Breathe in, breathe out.

Hands steadier, I took my purse to the sink and touched up my make-up. My face didn't need anything but it gave me something to do. I dawdled a couple more minutes then returned to our table. I chickened out the instant I saw him.

"I'm leaving."

Instead of arguing with me, he leaned back in his chair, crossing his arms over his chest. "Of course you are."

What was that supposed to mean? "Excuse me?"

"You're upset. When people are angry or upset, it's because they feel deep emotions. Only strong feelings can bring about such negative behavior. You're leaving because seeing me has brought out deep feelings in you."

"Wow, Professor, tell me more." I rolled my eyes, but inside I cursed him.

"If you held no animosity toward me, you'd stay and listen what I have to stay. But I guess that's not the case, is it?"

Reverse psychology. He looked so smug, I wanted to slap him. Instead, I took my seat and casually crossed my legs. I folded my hands in my lap and calmly met his gaze. We probably had a good twenty minutes before our food arrived, but I swore I wouldn't be the first one to break the silence.

"You're even more beautiful than I remember."

The nerve of this guy was unbelievable. So he wouldn't suspect his affect on me, I rolled my eyes and snatched up my phone again, opening my email. Thankfully, Logan let me have some peace while I replied to emails.

The surly waitress set a plate in front of me and the aroma tickled my nose. My mouth watered. "Thank you," I told her, but Marcia ignored me. To my great relief, for the next few minutes Logan only opened his mouth to fill it with food and spared me the chore of participating in conversation.

I sampled the asparagus. "Oh, my God, this is so good." Eventually, we both ran out of food. I folded my napkin and started to stand. "Well, that was interesting. Since I've proven I'm perfectly capable of sitting across from you, and therefore have no strong feelings for you, I—"

"Do you know why exes become bitter?"

My mouth dropped open and I couldn't think of a good answer, so I stayed seated, unable to complete my departure.

"Because they loved so much, that's why." His

gray eyes gazed at me intently, his hand motionless beside his plate as though I'd fly away if he moved. "The thing is, if they loved each other once, they can love again. But I'm not sour, Shelby, because I never stopped loving you."

My hand jerked, rattling my fork against my plate. He actually looked like he was waiting for a response. Instead of giving him one, I rose on wobbly knees and headed for the entrance. I didn't worry about Logan chasing after me. It wasn't his style. His was the slow, gentle seduction — so slow that the girl ended up doing the seducing without even realizing it. Besides, he still had to pay the check.

I still reelied from his words and knew I hadn't seen the last of him. But I had something else on my mind.

Next stop, Ginny.

The door to Ginny's house swung open to reveal her husband, Victor. "Hey, Shelby. Ginny's in the shower but she'll be out in a minute. C'mon in."

I followed Victor through the kitchen, past the stick-figure crayon drawings stuck to the fridge. The four-year-old twins poked their heads out of the opening of a fort made from a cardboard box and grinned as I made my way into the living room. A football game blared from the TV. Victor would be lost in it again shortly and that was fine by me. I was saving my wrath for his wife anyway.

Forgoing the sofa, I ambled around the room admiring their family pictures. Ginny and Victor in Hawaii last summer with the twins. Ginny in a white dress and veil on their wedding day, Victor looking down at her adoringly. Setting the photo down, I tried to ignore the emptiness in my soul, the incompleteness. I'd never have what Victor and Ginny had, especially not with Logan. He and I were ancient history. It had taken me a very long time to get used to that concept. The last thing I needed was to be sucked in by his charm again, only to learn the same lesson all over again.

"I liked your colorful texts." Ginny grinned as she strolled past the television in a fuzzy pink robe, rubbing a towel through her honey blond hair. "How was your date?"

"You must be referring to the ambush at The Boat House?" I folded my arms over my chest, lifting one brow. "Why would you do such a thing? You know how I feel about him."

She stopped patting her hair. "Yes, I do know how you feel. Which is exactly why I did it. I thought maybe if you saw him again, you'd either get over it or get back together. It's a win-win situation."

"Ha!" My hands shot to my hips. "I don't need to get over him. I finished with him years ago." Okay, so it wasn't the whole truth but no one needed to know that. Certainly not my meddling best friend.

She gave me her do-you-really-think-I'm-going-to-buy-that look. "Is that why you spend three times longer on the Logan articles than any normal person, then throw the magazine away before you read the rest?"

"I do not." Sure, I did.

"Do so." Ginny put a hand on her own hip, brows raised. "Any time someone mentions his name, you're suddenly very interested in the conversation. And don't think I haven't noticed how you kept the promise ring he gave you."

I narrowed my eyes at her. "That ring is valuable. I'm saving it for a rainy day. In case I end up homeless or something."

She shrugged and it was as if I hadn't even spoken. "You never wear it but it's still in your jewelry box. Anyone else would have given it away by now. But you haven't. Because deep down, you still love him. It's the only thing that makes sense. It also explains why none of your relationships last."

She was right. The promise ring and old pictures of him should have been tossed ages ago. But I could never quite completely let go. I averted my eyes not to give myself away. "I dated the guy almost three years. It's only natural I'd save mementos of something that was a big part of my past."

"You don't fool me. So when he showed up the other day and pleaded his case, I figured if you saw him, maybe you could get some closure. I resorted to sneakiness only because I care." She tilted her head. "Please don't be mad at me."

Ginny had the face of an angel and matching

temperament, a heart of sunshine and daisies. If she did something, it was with the purest of intentions. I couldn't stay mad at her. But she needed to know that Logan and I had no future.

"I'm going to let you slide, but only because he obviously conned you. He was always good at making me believe he cared." I cut the distance between us for a quick hug. "Just don't do it again. It's all a lie, Ginny."

"Then there's no harm in talking to him. You're not the same naïve girl you were back then. You can take care of yourself this time around. If he's going to be a jerk, I know you'll make sure he eats it."

I laughed weakly. "I already tried, only he seemed to come out the winner of our little scramble."

"He won the battle, not the war. You'll get your chance." Ginny held my shoulders. "Just make sure if you hurt him, he actually deserves it now, not for ancient history."

Crap. I didn't want to have to watch out for his feelings. The only person I needed to protect was me — starting with therapy. Not the traditional kind, but my own personal brand. First, some stretches, then a five-mile run, followed by weights or yoga.

Physical exertion grounded me, centered my thoughts — and made me too tired to think of Logan. It's how I had survived the first few months after he left.

It's how I still survived and how I would get through Logan's trip home. He'd be gone soon enough and I'd go back to my lonely life.

Chapter Three

I sat in my office chewing on a pencil, trying to distract myself from remembering how yummy Logan had looked the night before. I'd barely gotten any work done since. Instead, I kept finding myself fiddling with the few items adorning my wide desk; rearranging the stapler, the paper clip bin and the small pink vase. But it was early still, just before ten, and I had plenty of time to get everything done.

Tina poked her head in my office and grinned just as I was booting up my computer. "You'll never guess who's waiting in reception for you. Logan Starks." Her eyes widened. "He wants you to show him some houses."

My mouth dropped open. The man was insane. Certifiable. Why was he stalking me?

I grimaced. "It's a scam. I'm not sure what he wants, but it's not for me to help him find a house."

"Not according to him." She narrowed her eyes. "When I asked him what he wanted, he'd done his homework. The man's serious, I'm telling you. In any case, I already assured him you're available so you're stuck. Do you know what kind of clients we'd bring in if we put him down on our resume?"

"Don't care," I chirped.

"Oh really? When was the last time you closed an escrow?"

I frowned. It wasn't my fault that all my recent clients had gotten cold feet. The house market was a bit shaky at the moment and people were leery. "I can live without a commission off Logan," I said slowly.

But Tina smiled tightly, looking like she was going in for the kill. "So you're that afraid of him? Do you really think he'll spend millions of dollars on a house just to what—? Date you? Sleep with you?"

When she put it that way, it did sound ludicrous. This was Logan after all. Big Hollywood stud. My face heated with embarrassment, but I tried not to let Tina make me do something I'd regret. "If he's a serious buyer, anyone can show him a house. If he just wants to get laid, he doesn't need me for that. Wendy's a huge fan and she's pretty. Give him to her." I rubbed at my temples. Why was Logan back? It was as if he'd been put on Earth to make me suffer.

Tina stretched taller and gave me a stern look. She ran an orderly office with high sales and she was the only one who worked more hours than me, even though I sold more. Usually. Still, I had the utmost respect for her. "He's asking for you. Are you saying you can't put your personal differences aside and be a professional?" she asked.

I groaned. How come it was always the injured party who had to be the adult and be professional? First, Logan had challenged me to have dinner with him and I'd given in. Now, Tina was throwing down the gauntlet. Obviously, fate was trying to tell me something.

"This is business, Shelby. And as your superior, I'm telling you that Logan Starks has been waiting out there long enough."

My pencil snapped between my fingers. "Fine." Maybe this was some sort of cosmic test. If I could face Logan and be a professional, maybe I'd pass and get to move on with my life.

I stomped out of my office and right up to Logan who stood at the receptionist's desk. By Janice's rapt expression, he'd probably been flirting with her. As if I wasn't annoyed enough already. I wanted to jab a finger into his chest. Instead, I smiled. "I understand you need help finding a house?"

Slowly, the corners of his mouth curled up. "I'll make it worth your while."

My stomach flipped and my eyes widened. While I was playing things professionally, his voice practically oozed sex. Handling him was like playing chess. I'd have to get better at anticipating his moves.

I spun on my heel and stormed back into my office. Of course, he was right behind me. By the time he'd taken a seat, I'd regained my composure. I typed my ID and password and logged into the site to search for houses. "What are you looking for specifically? Let's start with the area."

"Right down to business, huh?"

"Well, yes," I said, batting my eyelashes. "Unless you have another agenda. In that case, please feel free to clue me in."

"I told you my agenda last night, Shelby. I want you back."

"That's not going to happen. Now, if you really want a house, I can—"

"There was another girl."

The blunt words made me flinch.

"Sort of," he said softly.

"Sort of?" I choked out. How does one "sort of" have another girl? Either there is someone else or there isn't.

He stared at a paper clip as he reshaped it. "That's why I broke up with you. It wasn't because I didn't love you."

On the outside, I didn't move a muscle. But inside, my lungs wouldn't work, wouldn't inflate. So this was why he was here. To clear his conscience. "Is that supposed to make me feel better?" I felt suffocated.

"I... didn't sleep with her. She lived close by so we hung out a few times. I was still trying to work through the whole divorce thing. And my dad wasn't doing so good. I should have told you what was going on." His brows furrowed then his gaze fell to the broken pencil. "But I thought it would be easier for you if you didn't have to deal with... it."

It? "Lots of people deal with divorce, Logan. It's not an excuse to cheat."

"It wasn't just the divorce. My dad—"

"I don't care about your dad!" I hissed before slapping a hand over my mouth. Obviously, being professional was going to be a lot harder than I'd thought.

When he didn't say anything else, I took a deep breath and said, "Where do you want to live? In the heart of Sacramento or do you prefer a suburb?"

He looked frustrated. Like he wanted to keep talking about the past. I shook my head, giving him a silent message, You go there, and we're done.

Logan sighed. "A ten mile radius of my sister's house would be good."

Okay. Message received. It was a start.

"Square footage?" I tapped the keyboard, not bothering to glance at him.

"Uh... about the size of Kristin's house, I guess. Since it's just me."

"Two thousand square feet is small for a man of your celebrity status. What will Vivienne Martin say when she tears herself away from Hollywood?" I didn't give him a chance to answer. "Pool or spa?"

"Either way," he answered.

"Any preference on year built or lot size?"

"No."

"Price range and down payment?"

"No limit. Cash."

My greedy little heart went cha-ching. Then I remembered he had no intention of buying a house. His visit was a ruse and he was just wasting my time. I clicked search and waited for the real estate profiles to appear. "One story or two?"

He shrugged. "Doesn't matter."

"You sure it'll be big enough? Don't you want a home theater, a gym and five guest bedrooms for all your women and parties?" I was being bitchy but didn't care. I resented Logan for coming back into my life and bringing all my memories to the surface. It wouldn't have been so bad if I'd only remembered the bad, but the good times were also flitting through my head, reminding me how I'd felt about him when we were in love.

Logan looked to the ceiling as if God could help him. "Shelby, can you give it a rest?"

"Why don't you take your own advice, Logan, and go back to Hollywood," I said quietly.

"I could. But I'm not going to." He leaned forward. "Because I'm still in love with you. And whether you admit it or not, you're still in love with me."

"Ha!" I forced myself to laugh. "You've had groupies fawning over you for too long."

"Long enough to know I don't want them. I want you. Remember the night I gave you that ring?" Logan said, pausing a beat. "I'd been waiting for just the right moment to give it to you. When my parents told me I'd be living with my dad in LA, I knew it was now or never. Because I didn't want you to think, even for a second, that it was the end. I wanted you to wait for me."

How could I forget? I'd memorized the words the second they'd been formed.

We were sitting on the front porch steps, curled up against the cold and his arm around my shoulders. "I love you, Shelby. When I think about my future, whether I become a famous writer or a stay-at-home dad taking care of our kids so you can go off and conquer the world, it's always you and me. I can't picture my life without you. We may be living in different cities for a while, but we'll still be together."

I had leaned in and laid my head on his shoulder. He'd pressed me closer. Then I stood and took his hand. We snuck down the hallway and into my room.

A few soft words were all it took to fall into bed with him. I inwardly scoffed at my naivety so long ago.

I took a deep breath to ease the tension in my shoulders, returning my thoughts to the present and my gaze to the computer monitor. Obviously, my life would be so much easier if I told Logan to take a hike. But I knew he wouldn't go away. Maybe he was serious about buying a house. If he didn't work with me, then he'd work with another agent and he'd be around all the time anyway. If he ended up working with Emma or Maddie, I'd have to listen to them gush over him. I'd be even more distracted and I probably wouldn't be able to get my work done anyway.

I'd help him find his house, take my commission then cut ties — with a side benefit of proving to myself that I wasn't susceptible to him. "I had a crush on you as a girl, Logan. I'm over it. Let's move on. Are you serious about buying a house or not?"

"You loved me back then, Shelby. Real love, not a schoolgirl crush," Logan said.

"So you say," I said, making eye contact with him for only a moment before deliberately shifting to my computer monitor. He was wrong if he thought those old feelings meant anything now. I'd never let myself love him that way again and open myself up to the vulnerability, the pain. "Did you want to look at houses right away or will I have the opportunity to do something productive today?"

He cursed softly and ran his hands through his hair. Then he clapped his hands together, making me jump. "Okay, we'll play this your way. Let's go shopping. We can make a day of it. Lunch is on me." He smiled but it looked forced, like he'd gotten the hint.

I could only hope.

He signed the paperwork, officially making me his agent — no way would I put in the hours only to have him dump me as an agent too — and for the next half hour, we sorted through profiles and I printed out the more promising ones.

"We can call and make appointments while we're out." I rose and slung my purse over my shoulder.

"I never stopped loving you," he said as we both got to the door.

Liar. I whirled around and glared. "I was seventeen

and it's been nine years. We've both grown up. I'm not the same stupid kid and I won't be so gullible this time." Why did he keep drawing me into these conversations? "So far, Logan, you're all talk and no action. The story of your life. No follow-through." I tried to get past him but he blocked the door. I backed up when I noticed his eyes ablaze, thinking maybe I'd pushed him too far.

As if I were his prey, he caged me against the wall with his arms. I pressed my back into cold wall so I wouldn't feel his thighs brushing mine. He only moved closer, a breath away, the friction of our bodies sending an inferno through me.

Oh, yes, that had definitely been missing in my life.

"You want me to follow through, I'm ready right now," he growled softly.

Me too. But Logan was the last guy I'd go there with. Although it wouldn't exactly be a hardship re-enacting certain moments with someone that stunning, deep down I was still bruised by his past rejection.

But I couldn't deny I was tempted.

I'd never had a relationship that lasted. If I was doomed to a life of loneliness, it almost seemed justifiable to take happiness where I could find it, even if only temporarily.

Logan inched toward me, his lips at my temple. My pulse spiked as he sucked my earlobe between his lips and I shuddered.

"I knew you still loved me," he whispered in my ear.

His words slapped me back to reality. A temporary

fling with him would only bring me a lifetime of more pain. No. Way. "Oh, honey, you're confusing love with lust." I patted his cheek a little harder than necessary and pushed on his chest. "A guy like you should know better. Let's go eat. I'm hungry." I sailed past him knowing I'd thrown him a nice curve.

I'd just taken his bishop. Score one point for me.

We picked a restaurant near some of the houses that had caught Logan's interest. It was definitely one of the nicer restaurants around. If the meal were on me, I'd have picked some place with reasonable prices. I ordered a salad even though getting something expensive would have been more satisfying. No point in saving Logan's money. But the priciest thing on the menu, while undoubtedly rich in flavor, would also be rich in calories. If I gave into that temptation, once Logan left again, all I'd have to show for his visit would be a fat ass.

"This is nice. We should do this more, spend time together."

"I'd rather not." Head down and paper in hand, I pretended to be fascinated by one of the house profiles.

"If you want to limit our relationship, like you keep hinting at, hanging out with me shouldn't be a problem for you, if that's what you really want. Unless you're afraid you're going to fall in love with me again."

Sounded like a challenge. "Let me get this straight. I should hang out with you to prove I don't want to hang out with you?" I snorted. "I don't want to be around a pedophile either but I'm not going to do it just to prove the point."

He let out a quick laugh. "I'm just saying that if you really don't love me, helping me buy a house should be simple enough. But you're making this about as pleasant as drowning. It's not personal. Right?" He leaned closer, his voice lowering to a whisper. "Seems very personal to me."

He had that right. But explaining to him how personal it had been when he dumped me would only show how much I had loved him. It would also reveal how hard I had to work to keep those feelings in past tense. "You and I have entered into a business contract. You're the one who keeps making it personal." Hoping to cut off further conversation, I opened my phone and began setting up appointments until our food appeared.

"What do you think? It's nice, huh?" Logan opened a closet then closed it. "Lots of storage space."

The house probably looked even better to him after the last two stinkers we saw. But was he serious about buying? Even if he had no intention of ever living in Sacramento again, he could always rent it out. It's not as if a seven figure book advance, along with his take of a blockbuster movie, made it difficult to buy one small house. If nothing else, it was an investment. He'd probably go through with the purchase just to prove me wrong and I'd make the commission. If he tried to see me again, I'd say no to his advances. And continue to say no. Not because I didn't want to give him a second chance, I realized, but because deep down, despite my confident exterior and quick retorts, I was an insecure mess when it came to him.

Shutting him out completely would be less painful than letting him in, only to have him realize yet again that I wasn't so exciting after all. When he eventually left me, I wanted him to know he hadn't won this time. "Hardwood floors, crown molding, high ceilings. Pretty."

"Yeah." Logan stared out at the yard. "I think you're right though. Something a little bigger would be better. One day I might want a family and we'd need room for the kids."

We? My insides twisted. He meant his future wife, of course, whoever she may be. Him thinking of me when he said that was wishful thinking on my part. I averted my face and pretended to examine the double paned window so he wouldn't see my eyes mist.

I really needed to pull it together. Even if Logan wanted to settle down, he'd never do it with me. He'd already proven that once.

We viewed a couple more houses then I dropped him off at his car in the parking lot of my office. Being with Logan and keeping up the barrier had drained me. I just wanted to go home.

That evening, I ran six miles which was a little more than usual. Even that didn't burn off my frustration. Why did he have to come back and disturb my peaceful world? I could only hope he found a house quickly.

To wind down, I walked the last block. One thing I hated about working out was how you seemed to sweat more after you stopped running. Annoying. My yoga pants clung to my ass and sweat trickled between my breasts. My breathing slowed and I glanced at my house. Someone was taking up space on my front porch steps. Someone male. Someone with dark hair and who was impossibly gorgeous.

Chapter Four

Logan looked up and smiled. "Hey."

My heart betrayed me by skipping a beat. "Please tell me you're not stalking me."

His brows lowered for only an instant before he smiled. "I just stopped by to give you something."

"Is it money?" Better for him to think I'm greedy than bitter from unrequited love. Maybe he'd believe it enough and stop trying to lure me in.

"No, but it might bring money in one day. To me anyway." He held out a two-inch bundle of papers.

My brows rose and I put my hands on my hips.

"It's uh… it's my latest manuscript."

Now that was a surprise. "And you're giving it to me why?"

"Because every time I try to talk to you about anything other than houses, you shut me down. So… just read it. Maybe you'll get a new perspective."

That meant the manuscript was about our past. No thanks. "I'm not much of a reader. Listen, I still have calls to make. I'll text you later when I know what time our first appointment is tomorrow." Please leave before I throw myself at you. I held my arms stiff at my sides so I wouldn't reach out to him.

"Uh, sure." He left the steps and walked the narrow concrete path to his waiting black Jaguar.

Good. I didn't want him inside my house. Too cozy. Too tempting. Not one to take chances, I waited until he drove away to go inside. As I stepped up onto the porch, I spied the bound stack of paper. Damn, he'd left the manuscript. I'd been so intent on keeping my distance and getting him to leave that I hadn't noticed he'd laid it down.

Snatching it, I went inside and slipped it under the sofa.

My heart sputtered when I got Logan's text the next day.

I'll pick you up at 9.

No way. If we drove in Logan's car, I'd be trapped and at his mercy all day. Who knew where he'd take me against my will. My hands raced across the keyboard of my cell. Either we drive both cars from house to house or just my car. Those are your only two choices.

Fine. I'll b ready and waiting at my house.

Too bitchy. From now on, I'd play it a little cooler,

act indifferent. Maybe then he'd go away. Preferably before I broke down and jumped him. Before I had the chance to ask him for his address, he texted it to me.

At precisely nine, I cruised into a middle class neighborhood and rolled into the driveway of your average house. Why wasn't he at a hotel with room service or at least a richer neighborhood?

I'd foolishly hoped he'd be waiting outside so I wouldn't have to come in. Grinding my teeth, I parked behind his Jag and knocked on the front door. And waited. I knocked again.

The door swung open to reveal Logan, a big fluffy green towel wrapped around his hips and little drops of water glistening over his bare chest. He'd filled out. And then some. He looked like he worked hard at the gym but liked a good meal too, the end result being the perfect combination of bulk and definition.

We definitely weren't in high school any more.

He motioned for me to come inside. "My agent called and wanted to go over some revisions before we submit a project to my editor. Sorry. I'll be a couple more minutes." He disappeared, leaving the door open, obviously expecting me to follow.

Oh, hell.

I crept past the door and shut it, my eyes wandering to the entryway and beyond into the startlingly clean living room. Either he had a regular maid or he'd just moved in that morning. A maid was more likely.

Water rushed through the pipes as he ran it in the

bathroom, obscuring any sounds I made. I took the opportunity to explore the house and see how Logan lived. The master bedroom loomed ahead and I crept toward it. A button down shirt covered the back of a chair and a pair of jeans was strewn across an unmade bed. The indented pillow and rumpled sheets hinted that someone had recently slept there. A half full glass of water, a wallet and car keys lay on the dresser. I tiptoed closer.

Glancing at the adjoining bathroom, I saw shadows move beyond the partially open door. I glanced at his wallet again, wondering how many pieces of paper I'd find from women who'd slipped him their number. Snooping like that was beneath me but I needed to know if he was lying when he said he loved me. I had to have proof. My peace of mind depended on it.

Gingerly, I picked up the wallet and opened it. It was crammed with little pieces of paper, notes and credit cards. I carefully pulled out a tiny yellow slip of paper, making a mental note of where it belonged. Angela 555-4698. And another with Lisa 555-9182. Then three more just like those. Granted, women threw numbers at guys like him all the time but why would he keep them if he had no intention of using them? For all I knew, he had a date with one of them later that day. I squeezed my eyes shut, trying to wash away the hurt.

I stuffed the papers back in his wallet, not really caring anymore how they'd been arranged before. I'd gotten my evidence but it didn't bring the relief or closure I'd hoped for.

At the door creaking open, I closed his wallet and dropped it on the desk.

"Hey."

I flinched and my hand hit the glass and water spilled over the shiny surface of the dresser. "Damn it."

A moment later, he brought a hand towel and sopped up the water.

"Sorry," I said.

"No problem. I'm glad you did that."

"Made a mess on your dresser? Seriously?"

He laughed. "I was beginning to think you'd become this hard woman with nerves of steel. You getting nervous around me proves I can still get to you."

I couldn't let him see how flustered he got me. "What? What?" The echo was not helpful.

"You remind me of a girl I once knew. Sweet and innocent. Every time I looked at her, I thought I was seeing an angel," he whispered, moving close enough to tuck a strand of hair behind my ear. His proximity excited my senses, confused my brain. My body tensed, anticipating what I was pretty sure would be a damn good ride.

Not going to happen. I backed up and he closed the distance again.

"I couldn't talk to you after I kissed that girl. I was afraid you'd figure out I wasn't good enough for you and dump me. Waiting for the ball to drop was torture." His thumb brushed my temple and I pulled away.

"So you dumped me instead? I would have forgiven you. The fact that you blew me off is what made you not good enough for me. And news flash. You don't make me nervous. Getting caught rifling through your wallet to see if you have a dozen girls' phone numbers, which you do, is what made me jump. I'll wait for you out there." I bolted.

Pictures lined the hallway walls and I paused for a closer look. A man and woman surrounded by three kids smiled at me.

Peppermint and something else not unpleasant assaulted my senses, sending a stab of unwanted desire through my gut.

"Friends of mine. They're gone for the summer so I rented it out."

I sidestepped, hoping to escape Logan and the sexy scents of clean yumminess, making me want to lick him all over. I needed to resist those impulses. I couldn't stand it if I gave in then he went for one of the girls who wrote their numbers on tiny pieces of paper for him.

"Why here and not a swanky hotel?"

"Hotels are so impersonal. I'm lower maintenance than you think."

Yeah, he didn't require much. He certainly hadn't needed me nine years ago. "Ready to go?" I asked, keeping my gaze off him.

"All set."

Inside my car, I started it up then glanced over to find Logan grinning. "What?"

"Going through my wallet was an invasion of privacy, don't you think?"

Then why was he smiling? "You don't look too broken up over it."

"I'm not, but only because you were seeing if there were other women. Which only proves you do care."

Caught. A part of me really hated him at that moment.

"Or maybe I wanted evidence so I could once and for all prove what a player you are. Then maybe, just maybe you'd give up." Ouch. That was cruel, even for a woman scorned.

He didn't even twitch. His eyes didn't waver. "Nah. I gave up once, long ago. It didn't work out too well for me. Besides, those numbers don't mean anything. When someone gives me their number, it's not like I'm going to throw it away right in front of them. So I stuff it in my wallet and forget about it. If I intend to call a girl, her number goes straight into my cell."

I heard the tiny little explosion in my head as my evidence went poof. Sadly, it wouldn't do any good to snag his phone and sneak a peek at his contacts since I wouldn't know a potential date from someone at his publishing house.

As I signaled to leave the curb, my phone rang. Caller ID told me it was Jared.

He was probably in town for a few days and wanted to get together. I wished the thought brought me more pleasure. How could I go out with anyone after spending time with Logan? But answering the call would get me out of the awkward turn our conversation had taken. I pulled over again and took the phone off blue tooth, since I didn't want my conversation overheard by Logan. "Excuse me a second." I hit the button on my phone and answered, "Hello?"

"Hey, babe, it's me."

I cringed at the familiar term. Normally that endearment would've been fine from Jared, but not since Logan showed up. "I'm in town and was wondering what you're doing tonight."

"Oh, uh..." Thoughts of getting together with Jared seemed so remote now. It felt like I'd dated him months ago instead of only weeks. Until the Logan invasion, I'd thought Jared was pretty hot. Maybe he was exactly what I needed to purge Mr. A-lister from my head. "Going out with you, of course."

"Great. Pick you up at seven?"

Logan's scowl crept into my peripheral vision and I turned to get him out. "Sure. See you at seven." I hung up.

"Making a date with Jared, I see. What does he do?"

Little needles pricked at my skull, threatening a migraine of mammoth proportions. The two men were giving me a headache. I pulled away from the curb, hoping we weren't going to be late and that the selling agent would still be there. "Well, he's not a fancy writer hobnobbing with celebs and jet-setting across the country."

"But you didn't answer the question." Logan swiveled in the passenger seat to watch me.

"He's a doctor."

"How did you meet him?"

Why did Logan care? Or was he just trying to get a rise out of me? My bunched up shoulders were beginning to cramp. Logan was not healthy for me. Maybe if I quit resisting so hard, he'd quit pushing. "I helped him buy an investment property a couple months ago."

"Oh." Logan's brows furrowed. "You don't strike me as the type to date your clients. You're too much of a pro for that kind of thing. You'd wait until your business is finished. Which tells me you haven't been dating him long. "

Just great. Now I couldn't even pretend I was in a serious relationship. "Right."

Out of the corner of my eye, I saw Logan's triumphant smile, which was both annoying and confusing. "I don't get it." I stopped at the red light and whipped my head around to face him. "You could have any girl you want, someone prettier than me. But you're here, pursuing someone who's not exactly encouraging you."

"First, there's no one prettier than you." He held up one finger to silence me when I scoffed. "Second, you haven't made it clear at all. In fact, you've done the exact opposite. The more you try to make me believe you don't want me, the more convinced I am that you still love me."

"I give up trying to reason with you," I mumbled, blowing out a breath.

Several minutes later, we pulled up in front of the

first house of the day. A three thousand square foot Spanish style home, built in the early thirties. It had an arched entryway, curved ceilings, hardwood floors and it had been recently painted.

Logan poked his head into rooms and opened cabinets, finally stopping at the back door overlooking the garden. "Let's put in an offer."

The house was nice but Logan could do better. It wasn't as if he lacked funds and I couldn't imagine him looking forward to remodeling when he could be writing. "Really? I think we should look around a little more before you decide on anything."

One side of his mouth curled up. "Don't want to end our precious time together so soon?"

"Exactly, because I'm always rude and sarcastic to people I want to hang out with." I shook my head, knowing that if I let him buy the house, he'd be out of my life sooner. But I couldn't. It wasn't in me to let any client get a less than suitable house. "I like my clients to look around so they have things to compare it to. Gives you perspective. Then if something goes wrong with the deal, you already know the alternatives so you can make an informed decision."

"Thought you'd be happy for me to decide right away, get me out of your hair."

"I'd love nothing more, trust me. But you're my client." I shrugged. "I want to put you in a house you'll fall in love with. Besides, I can already tell it needs a new roof and you never know how willing the sellers will be to negotiate on the price. Let's go out and get you a Plan B and C."

◆ ◆ ◆

"Oh, wow, this is nice. Much better layout." Logan traveled the hallway of the vacant house, poking into rooms.

"And it's priced better too." I gloated. "This is exactly why we're going to look at a couple more. If you still want this house by then, we'll write the offer later this afternoon." My cell rang. "Hello?" I ogled Logan's muscular arms as he slipped out the back door.

"Ms. Winters, Wayne Fellows here."

"Oh, Mr. Fellows. How are you?"

"Not sure. I've been looking over the inspection report for the Meadowview property. I'm having second thoughts. Maybe that house needs too much work."

"We don't know that yet," I said in my most soothing voice. "Look, I want you happy with whatever you end up with but the reality is that all houses need work. And there aren't that many ten thousand square foot houses that meet your specs. Just hang on. The specialists will be there tomorrow. Let's see what they say before we cancel escrow, okay?"

There was a long pause and I bit the inside of my lip, wishing Mr. Fellows would chill. He'd probably never get another deal that good.

"Alright. I'll wait until tomorrow. See you then."

I hit the end button and exhaled.

"You have a buyer with cold feet, huh?"

I jolted. "Eavesdropper. You ready to look at the next one?"

"Sure." Logan held the front door open for me then trailed after me. "Must be a hefty commission on a house that big."

"That's not the point, Logan." I sighed, pressing the clicker to unlock my car. We got in and I twisted to face him. "He'd been burned before I met him, ended up with a couple money pits. We've been in escrow on three different houses and on this one for two months and I haven't made a dime. Now he's too scared to settle on anything. I've tried to assure him that the house is in good shape and the inspection report backs me up. But he's too paranoid to see that." I dropped my head against the back of the seat. "I'm willing to put in the time, but not without the hope of a payoff eventually."

"I get it. I'd love to hog you up for myself but if you need to go, I'll understand. We can look at those other houses tomorrow."

Logan's offer made me warm and fuzzy. I shook my head and started the car. "No. Can't do anything on the Fellows deal until tomorrow anyway."

Later that evening, we sat at Logan's dining room table reviewing the info on the houses we'd looked at. He pointed at a piece of paper.

"This one?" I held up the house profile he'd indicated.

"You're sure you don't want to look around more?"

Logan sat next to me, so close we rubbed arms, and narrowed his eyes thoughtfully. "What did you think of the house?"

Glorious. Breathtaking. "Doesn't matter what I think. But if I thought it was a crappy deal, I wouldn't let you do it."

He nodded. "Okay, but what do you like about that house? What's special about it?"

I smiled dreamily. "It's... it's not so much about glamour, although the house has that, for sure. It's a matter of comfort too even though it's bigger than you were looking for. The master bedroom is near the other bedrooms, but not too close. You could keep an ear on children while not hearing too much. With the French doors off the dining room, you can pick up your coffee and the newspaper right after breakfast and catch a breeze on the balcony. It's little comforts like those that make a real home. Plus, it's on a huge lot so there's plenty of privacy." I paused, remembering the lush landscaping. "I don't know. There are so many things to love about it."

"If you could afford a house like that, I'd be in a bidding war with you right now."

I snorted. "No, you wouldn't. Because if I had a real chance at that house, you'd never have the opportunity to see it."

Logan laughed and caught a hank of my hair between his fingers. "We should do dinner. You must be hungry."

I'd been treating him like anyone else the past several hours. More than that — I'd been treating him like a friend. Ever since Mr. Fellows threw me for a loop. Logan had slipped right in. Our conversations had been easy, as though we'd never parted. He wasn't my friend though. I needed to remember that. I lifted a shoulder to brush him off. "I have a date, remember?"

His lips tightened. "Right. You're seeing the doctor tonight."

I grabbed my files, headed to the door and kept my voice void of any emotion. "I'll get your offer written up and I'll be back in the morning for a signature."

Chapter Five

For my date with Jared, I wanted to wear something that shouted just friends. We had kissed on our last date and it had been nice enough to make me want more. Until Logan showed up. Naturally, Jared would expect more of the same tonight. A few more dates and we might've had sex. Too bad Logan's return to town threw everything off.

I rejected the little red dress and stilettos, opting for low heels, black pants and a soft grey scoop-neck blouse.

What was I doing? I should call Jared and cancel. It wasn't fair to go out with a guy while thinking about another. The idea of doing that to Jared made me feel dirty. Checking my watch, I realized he was probably half way to my house. By the time I finished explaining why we shouldn't go out, he'd be at my front door. Ending it with someone in person was more personal and less cold anyway.

Up the road when my business with Logan concluded I'd have no romantic prospects. Who knew when another eligible guy would come along? I wasn't the kind of girl who slept with a guy on the first date... or second. It could be months before I had a chance at sex again. Sometimes, doing the right thing sucked. I whimpered at the prospect of the long dry spell. Heck, I was already in one.

The doorbell rang fifteen minutes early. Creeping to the front door, I checked the peephole half expecting to see Logan. Much to my disappointment and relief, Jared stood on the other side, his blond hair spiked up and big beefy shoulders seeming to stretch to both sides of the front porch.

Still, my heart didn't beat faster for Jared, despite his rugged good looks. "Hi," I said, a smile ready as I let him in.

"Hey." He bent for a kiss and I leaned forward to hug him instead, releasing him quickly.

His eyes narrowed. "What's wrong?"

I shut my eyes and took a deep breath. "I'm really sorry. We can't go out."

"Are you sick?" He laid a hand on my forehead. Always the doctor.

"It's nothing physical. It's..."

"What happened? Are you okay?"

"More like who happened, not what," I said and he raised his brows. "Can I get you something to drink, since you're here?"

"Beer, if you have one." He followed me into the kitchen.

I popped the cap and handed him the bottle. "My ex boyfriend came into town and he's ruining my life."

"Exes come and go." Jared shrugged then studied my face. "What's the problem? Is he stalking you or something? I know someone in the police department."

A quick flash of Logan being arrested gave me a sort of satisfaction but I cared too much for him to ever let him get hurt. "No, it's nothing like that. I got stuck working with him on a real estate deal." I flopped onto one of the wood chairs.

"Ah, I see." Jared sighed. "You're still in love with him."

I scoffed. "No, I'm not."

He sat next to me and bumped my shoulder. "Yes, you are."

"I hate him." I dropped my head back and stared at the ceiling.

Jared chuckled.

"He's not good for me. Logan equals pain."

"Logan?" Jared asked.

Oops. I hadn't meant to give Jared a name. But he wouldn't know it was the Logan, local celebrity. "Just some guy. You probably don't know him."

"What did he do to make you hate him? I have to be sure never to do that."

I got up and grabbed myself a beer. Why not? This way, if Jared prodded too much and I got emotional, I could literally cry in my beer. I'd been doing it metaphorically anyway. "You'd have to let me fall madly in love with you, cheat on me, then dump me. Easy."

"Well, whoever he is, he's stupid. How about you and I hang out anyway? I prefer my women in love with me so you're safe. We already have the beer so now we just need pizza. What do you say?"

I beamed. "I downloaded a movie earlier."

If I'd never known Logan, I could have easily settled in comfortably with Jared. He was everything I wanted in a man — gorgeous, successful, confident and fun. Guys like that didn't come around too often. But he wasn't a prospect for me. Not now. Not until I could forget the Logan I knew long ago. That kind of love was what I missed, what I wanted to have again.

But it would never be with Logan. I'd always be wondering how long I had with him, when he'd leave again... whose number was in his wallet. I couldn't create a future with a guy I couldn't depend on for the long haul.

Jared had been a godsend. If not for him, I would have moped all night. I'd rented a drama but it was so badly done, we laughed through most of it. It almost took my mind completely off him.

The next morning, I stopped at the curb in front of Logan's house and grabbed the documents. Just before I got to the front door, he opened it and waved me in.

"How'd your date go last night with, uh... Jared? That was his name, right? Did he take you some place nice? Have fun?" He rapid-fired the questions as I stepped into the entryway.

I cocked my head. "Jealous?"

"A little." He folded his arms over his chest. "Okay, a lot."

I believed him. But that wasn't enough for me.

Scanning the living room for a flat surface, I found the coffee table. "You ready to sign?"

"Absolutely." He joined me, kneeling on the floor.

"If they accept your offer and we open escrow, you'll need to make the good faith deposit."

"No problem." Logan diligently signed every place I indicated then I stuck the papers back in the folder and stood.

"I'll get these emailed later today and let you know as soon as I hear from them."

"Okay." He shadowed me as I made a dash for the exit. "But you didn't answer my question."

"What question?"

"How was your date? Where did he take you?"

"Uh..." I looked down at my toes. Logan was being way too nosy. I could tell him to mind his own business but he'd only be more certain that I loved him. "We decided to stay in."

Logan's eye twitched. "The whole night?"

I'd never tell Logan that Jared and I were no longer romantically involved — or why. "No. He left early since he sees morning patients. Do you want the blow-by-blow, everything we did last night?" I lifted my chin, daring him to push but hoping he wouldn't.

"No." He shifted his weight to his other foot. "That was plenty."

I slogged into the office and sunk into my chair, leaned back and closed my eyes.

The specialty inspections had gone fairly well, better than most houses. But Mr. Fellows wouldn't see it that way. I could feel a cancellation coming on. Again.

Glancing at my monitor, I saw an email from the listing agent of Logan's house. Crap. It had been less than twenty-four hours since I'd sent Logan's offer to the other realtor and I'd already gotten an answer. If I'd been less efficient and faxed it the next morning, I could have dragged out the entire process and possibly had a forty-eight hour break from Logan. Long enough to get over him.

Who was I kidding? I couldn't totally get over him in nine years, much less two days. And poor pathetic me couldn't wait to see Logan to give him the news. Calling him would be healthier for me. But I always met my clients in person to go over the terms. I couldn't give Logan any less. Besides, if he accepted the counter-offer, he had to sign off on it. I had to see him that morning whether I wanted to or not.

I picked up the phone to call him but it rang before I got to it. I cursed my heart for jumping at the prospect of Logan calling me.

It was Mr. Fellows.

"I'm sorry, Shelby, but I'm canceling escrow. The combined total for the electrical, the roof and chimney repairs could be forty to sixty grand to fix everything. I didn't sign on for a fixer."

My stomach dropped. All that hard work for nothing.

Hearing a knock in the doorway to my office, I looked up to see Logan. I held up a finger so he would give me a minute and he leaned against the doorjamb. I turned away from the beautiful and distracting man to give Mr. Fellows my full attention.

"You figured it needed a little bit of work when we put in the offer. We knew about the roof from the beginning and the sellers warned you about the wonky electrical. I'll admit the chimney issues are a surprise but even if you spent forty grand on that, it's pretty minor considering you're buying a house for 2.5 million that appraised for over three."

My eyes stung. I'd been babying Mr. Fellows for months and months. I thought we'd finally found the right house and I'd worked so hard, put in so many hours, all to have it cancel for some stupid reason.

"You're saying I shouldn't worry about a few grand? Maybe if it was your money, you'd think differently," he snapped.

"No, that's not what I meant. Look, why don't we put in a request for repairs or ask them to give you a credit? See what they say."

"Fine. Do that." He hung up.

I buried my face in my hands. "Stupid man," I mumbled.

"You okay?" Logan asked.

I'd forgotten he was there. "Yes, I'm fine. Just frustrated is all."

"Lance Fellows, right?"

"Yeah."

"The guy's huge in the car industry. Owns most of the dealerships around here. You'd think he'd never bought a house before."

"Oh, he has. That's the problem. He's been burned." I shook my head. "I was just about to call you. Have a seat." I printed out the counter offer and handed it to him. "It's a fair deal."

He didn't answer, just picked up a pen and swept it along the signature line. When he'd initialed the last spot, he slid the papers across the table toward me. "Let's celebrate."

I stood and walked to the door as a hint that business was concluded. "Nothing to celebrate yet. As Mr. Fellows has proved over and over, the deal isn't done until escrow closes."

"Let's go out anyway." He rose and stood toe-to-toe with me.

"No, Logan. I'm not interested. I'd think you'd want your women willing." My insides knotted when his scent reached my nose, a mixture of after-shave and soap. "I'll stop by tomorrow and get your deposit check then I'll open escrow."

"Willing?" he asked. "You love me. You want me. The only reason the willingness is lacking is because you believe I don't return your feelings. But I do. I love you, Shelby."

"I judge people by what they do, Logan. And all I know is that we were in love, or so I thought, and you dumped me. You also kissed some random girl and didn't have the guts to tell me. If you want to convince me how sincere you are, then prove it."

The next instant, he pulled me to him by my waist with one hand, reached behind my neck with the other and dove. His mouth closed over mine and I opened as if in a trance, my tongue delving into territory all too familiar.

The years melted away as if he'd never been gone. Sweet memories rushed me and I wanted to relive them. I pushed myself against him, taking the kiss deeper. Logan spun us around and bumped my back into the wall. A tiny yelp of pleasure escaped my throat and my pulse quickened as his lips found my neck and my hands snaked up his shirt to touch those delicious abs.

But it wasn't enough. I wrapped my arms around his waist and pressed his hips against mine. Heat coursed threw me and I almost moaned.

"I love you, Shelby," he whispered in my ear.

Crap. Back to reality. I flattened my palms against his stomach and pushed. "No, you don't."

"I do. And that kiss just proved how much you love me."

I snorted. "You're not that naïve. If every steamy kiss meant true love, people would be getting married left and right."

"Ouch." He covered his heart with one hand. "Cold hearted."

"You made me that way. I'll see you tomorrow." Snatching my purse, I headed out on wobbly knees, praying he wouldn't follow. If he pushed any more today, he'd see what a fraud I was.

At the end of escrow, once Logan had the keys to his new home, I'd be done with him. Except that Logan's persistence and what appeared to be sincerity had already gotten to me. Again. Whether I fled the country or stayed in Sacramento, my heart would still break because he'd still dump me. Since my fate was sealed, it almost didn't matter if I slept with him or not. At least sex with him would give me an outlet for my frustration. But the sting of being dumped would increase tenfold by having completely given myself to him in that way again.

No, I would not sleep with Logan Starks again. My broken heart would heal faster with my pride intact.

Chapter Six

"It's Saturday and you're working?" Ginny asked.

"Yeah, I need to get Logan in escrow, or at least get the paperwork done so they'll open first thing Monday, then I have to see if I can save the Fellows deal." I groaned. "He's such a nice guy but he's torturing me."

"I always thought Logan was nice."

"No, not Logan." I rolled my eyes even though Ginny couldn't see me through the cell phone. "Mr. Fellows. He's about to cancel escrow."

"Again?" Ginny squeaked.

"Not if I can help it. I'll come by around noon," I said.

"Great. What's your agenda? Shopping, nails or lunch?"

I grinned. "How about all of the above?"

Ginny laughed. "See you then. And don't think you're getting out of spilling all the details on you and Logan."

"There is no me and Logan." I hung up and got to work.

The escrow company didn't work on Saturdays but Logan didn't know that. If he was bluffing, I wanted to know today rather than wait two days until Monday. Much to my surprise, when I arrived on his doorstep, Logan had the good faith deposit already written and waiting. I'd half expected him to try to delay me but when I turned to go, all he said was goodbye.

Strange. He didn't look beaten down or dejected. Or hostile. Just... preoccupied. He probably had another woman waiting. An actress come to visit him, more likely. Regardless of the mystery woman's profession, Logan had changed his mind about me already. I shouldn't have any feelings about that. And I didn't. The only thing I felt was emptiness... a big hole in my heart that might not close this time, never heal.

I went back to the office, called Mr. Fellows to discuss the figures and confirm his request, then typed it up. "Remember, today's Saturday. I seriously doubt they'll reply before Monday. Let's just hang tight, okay?"

He agreed and my breath whooshed out in relief. If he changed his mind and called to cancel, I wouldn't answer my phone. Even workaholics needed time to decompress once in a while. For the rest of the weekend, I was just a regular girl.

I turned off my computer, locked up and left my work behind me.

At the mall, Ginny and I hit our favorite stores.

"What made you do it, Ginny? How did Logan make you a believer?" I held up a red blouse and examined the fabric.

"Believer in what?" she asked. "Oh, that color will look fabulous on you."

"That he loves me. After what he did?" I added the blouse to the to-be-tried-on stack.

"Maybe he had his reasons, Shel. Have you talked to him about it yet?" She eyed a pair of jeans then moved on.

"What's the point? He dumped me. End of story."

"Maybe there's more to that story."

"Ginny, seriously?" We'd gone shopping to relax but the topic was undoing all the calm I'd collected over the last hour. My shoulders stiffened and I took a deep breath.

She stopped skimming the racks to study me. "I'd been a third wheel with you two for years. I watched you guys a lot and I'm telling you, Shel, that boy was madly in love with you."

"Then he left. Now there's a string of women."

Ginny scoffed. "Please. That's only according to the tabloids. Just because he's seen with a woman doesn't mean he's sleeping with her. Do you sleep with every guy you talk to?"

She had me there. A flash of Logan's kiss the day before invaded my brain, making me feel twitchy. "This topic is not exactly therapeutic. Can we talk about something else?"

She smiled. "For now. Let's go to the fitting room."

By the end of the day, we'd eaten too much to fathom fitting into our new clothes but our toes glittered. Ginny leaned over from the passenger side and hugged me when I pulled up in front of her house. "Go do your workout or whatever else, then come back for the party around eight, okay?"

I hugged her back. "I had fun today."

"Me, too." She smiled and got out of the car.

"Hey, Gin?"

She paused and turned back to face me.

"You didn't invite Logan, did you?"

She chuckled. "For someone so intent on not getting involved with him, you sure do give him lots of time in your head."

My brows drew together. "Did you?"

Ginny shook her head and closed the car door. "No. But it's my birthday and I want to have fun. I've invited quite a few people and some of them know Logan. I wouldn't put it past him to weasel an invite from somewhere. It's what I'd do if I was a man in love." At that she grinned and took off.

Crap. Everyone around here knew Logan, hometown boy who made it big. Ditching my best friend's birthday party was out of the question. I could only hope that he found something more exciting to do.

If I had any chance at all of seeing Logan tonight, I wanted to look my best. I slipped into my favorite pair of jeans then chose the skimpiest tank top I could find. Which wasn't that skimpy since I generally didn't go for the slutty look. But it rode up my hips just a bit to show my abs I'd worked so hard on. After straightening my hair, I added soft waves and fluffed it up. Just a little eye makeup and a touch of lip gloss and I surveyed my reflection. Not bad. Not bad at all.

As soon as I walked through the door of Ginny's house, what did my eyes behold? Logan and Jared. Talking. To each other. Well, good — easier to avoid both of them if they're together. But why were they conversing? Did they already know each other?

Logan spotted me almost as soon as I crossed the threshold, followed by Jared. Each lifted his glass at me and smiled. Crap. They had to have been talking about me.

"Shelby! Finally." Ginny hugged me as though we hadn't just seen each other a couple hours ago. "I was beginning to wonder if you'd changed your mind." She nodded toward the two hottest guys in the room. "Or bolted once you saw them."

"I must admit, the thought did cross my mind," I said, my mouth twitching.

"Don't you dare." Ginny wagged a finger at me. "It's my birthday."

"If I did bail, it would be your own fault for letting those two in." I raised one brow.

"What's wrong with Jared? I thought you two had fun the other night."

"Yeah, but don't you think it's kinda creepy that they're both over there ogling me?"

"Awkward, yes." She grinned then patted my shoulder. "You're gonna have to toughen up."

"That seems to be my life story right now."

"You could end it. Just takes one word — yes." She jerked her head toward the kitchen. "Let's get you a drink."

I followed her but waited until we'd passed the hotties to ask her what she meant. "End it? What do you mean exactly?"

"Sleep with Logan. Then you'd either get him out of your system and move on to Jared or you'd get inspired to work it out with Logan." She glanced over at the two men again. "I don't see how you can lose."

So tempting, but... "I dunno. Sounds risky. Don't think I could handle Logan dumping me again."

Inside the kitchen, she grabbed orange juice and vodka. "He won and you lost. Something happens to a person when they get dumped. It's hard on the psyche, even if we're planning on breaking up with him anyway."

Since when did my best friend become so insightful?

"You guys were just kids then," she continued. "But now, you're a grown woman. You're successful, confident and you have the tightest butt I've ever seen. Who can blame a guy for pursuing you? But this time around with Logan, you can be in control. And there might be benefits." She grinned.

Chuckling, I snatched the glass from her hand. "You are so bad."

She gazed into the liquid of her own glass. "I've been dumped by more than a few. And each time, it hurt like hell. But I know you love Logan. So reel him in."

"Victor's been letting you watch too many chick flicks." I rolled my eyes and took a sip of my screwdriver. "Love does not conquer all. And it doesn't justify everything. Besides, I'm not good with head games."

"Whatever gets you out of this weird limbo so you can get on with your life." Ginny studied me a moment. "Look, he was an eighteen year old boy. Who hasn't made at least one gross lapse in judgment as a kid? That's why God invented second chances."

What she was saying made sense but... "I don't know, Gin. My head goes in that direction more often than you'd think. But I don't ever want to go through that kind of pain again."

"Just make sure you're not missing out on something amazing just because you're a coward." Ginny reached behind her back and grabbed the vodka, uncapped it and poured more in my glass.

"No." I laughed and tipped the bottle back up. "Trying to get me drunk?"

"Yes. But I must tend to my guests, so go chat with the guys. If you don't, they'll know you're avoiding them."

"Why should I care if they know what I'm doing?"

"You don't want to burn both those bridges, do you?" she whispered in my ear with a giggle. "I live vicariously through you."

I laughed as Ginny vanished into the crowd. Leaving the kitchen, I searched for the duo. There they were, talking to a very pretty young blonde. And by the expression on her face, she was in heaven. I did a double-take. Ah, yes. Tiffany. I remembered comparing my abs to hers at the gym and feeling that mine weren't nearly cut enough. I also remembered how she worked the men, flirting with them mercilessly. She spent more time with the rich ones, guys I'd sold big houses to.

Neither Logan nor Jared were an option for me but that didn't mean I wanted to see Tiffany's claws in either of them. Jared was a good man, through and through. A guy like that might be susceptible to pure evil. Okay, I knew Tiffany wasn't evil. But I also knew she wasn't a nice girl.

Logan was used to handling women. If she made a move on him, he could take care of himself. And he wouldn't be heartbroken when it ended. But I didn't want to witness their coupling.

I made a bee-line for them.

"I didn't know you two knew each other," I told the boys.

"We met through his sister. We'd get invited to the same barbeques," Jared said. "I had no idea this was the Logan you were talking about."

Great. Now Logan knew I'd been talking about him on my date with Jared. No way would I let either of the boys steer me in that direction. Instead, I shifted to the blonde. "Nice to see you outside the gym."

"Yeah, I'm glad I came." She smiled in a way that made me suspect she might be part feline. I wouldn't be going near either of the two men if she had any say in it.

"Me, too." I smiled back and we stared at each other for several heartbeats.

Logan grinned, obviously amused at the interchange. "So, Shelby, how are you enjoying Ginny's birthday bash?"

"So far, so good. You?" I met his gaze with a challenge, mentally calculating how long before he ran off with the walking ad for fitness.

"Getting better." Logan grinned.

"Not from my perspective, but it will be in just a moment." I patted Jared's arm. "Maybe I'll see you later." I turned on my heel and strolled off. Feeling Logan's gaze on my ass, I congratulated myself on my choice of jeans and tank top. I looked fantastic in jeans.

Ginny stopped me just as I rounded a corner. "What was that all about?"

I beamed. "Just talking to them like you suggested."

She frowned. "Yeah, but I meant that you should let yourself go, get involved with Logan, take a chance. Not be bitchier."

Why was she pushing so hard? Maybe she thought Logan truly loved me and if I took up with him, I'd realize it too and we'd live happily ever after. Apparently, she needed a dose of reality. "You know what hurts the most?" I asked.

She shook her head.

"The betrayal. Logan was sweet, loving and patient, but he wasn't a kiss-ass either. He held his own with me and everyone else. He was everything a girl could want in a guy, but he was also my best friend. When he touched me, I knew he loved me with his whole heart and the world just fell away. When he left, it made me doubt everyone and everything." My chin trembled. "I can't go there again, Ginny. I just can't. Not with anyone."

"Okay," she said softly. "No more setting you up with him. This was the last time."

"So you did invite him?" More matchmaking attempts?

"Absolutely not! I knew you'd ask me and I didn't want to lie. I made Victor do it."

I laughed and hugged her. "This is why I love you."

She squeezed then released me. "Go mingle. Have some fun."

"Maybe I can help with that." Logan invaded my peripheral vision.

I turned to give him a quick scowl and when I turned back, Ginny had vanished. Figures.

"I doubt that," I said.

He held up both hands. "How about a truce? I don't tell you how much I love you and you dance with me. Just like regular friends."

I feigned boredom, looking around the room. "Not sure if that's possible for either of us. Serial dumping is your thing and avoiding disaster is mine." As if I wasn't guilty of dumping my share of guys. Logan wouldn't know that though.

He moved in front of me to catch my roaming gaze. "I don't love you and I don't want you back. Ever. You're much too... independent for me." The corners of his mouth curled up. "Dance?"

I tuned in to a ballad playing. A slow dance would require his hands on me. "I'll pass."

Glancing over, I spotted Jared and little Miss Yoga. They looked like they were really hitting it off. I grimaced.

"You don't want him but you don't want anyone else to have him either?" Logan asked.

"Who says I don't want him?"

"If you did, you wouldn't have told him you didn't want to see him anymore because you're ex was back in town. Me."

I snorted. "You? Right. Don't flatter yourself. I have plenty of other exes."

Logan looked cocky. "You mentioned me by name."

Oh, yeah. Hell. And damn Jared for spilling it. "You promised we wouldn't talk about us."

"So I did." He nodded and mimed zipping his lips. "Sorry."

"Jared's a great guy. I'd love to see him with a nice girl. But she's not a nice girl."

"Agreed." He chuckled. "Shall we break it up?"

"He's a grown man. I'm sure he can handle himself." Although joining Jared and the blonde seemed a better option than staying alone with Logan. Just the two of us. No matter how yummy that sounded, I knew it wouldn't end well.

"Let's join them anyway. You distract him and I'll pretend to hit on her."

"Pretend?" Oh, right, like I really wanted to watch him do that.

"Hey now." Logan looked offended. "We're being friends tonight, not exes. And even if I was interested in her, which I'm not — I like my women a little less fake and self-centered. And anyway, no guy in his right mind could think about her when you're in the room."

Fake. That was me, pretending I didn't want Logan. Not that I intended to change my ways. I just wanted him to see the flaw in his logic. "And that's why you're hanging out with me, because I'm so considerate and generous."

"You don't fool me. I know beyond the quips, the insults and all that professionalism on the job, there's still the generous and loyal girl I fell in love with."

"It's been a long time, Logan. What you see now is what you get." I took a sip of my drink and shifted slightly so I could people-watch.

"What I've seen is how you treat other people, how you want to help them. You don't let your personal feelings get in the way of your principles. You want to make that commission off Mr. Fellows. You want it so bad you can smell the money. But you'd give it up in a heartbeat if you didn't think he was getting a fair deal. You could have let me buy that first house and been rid of me sooner but you didn't. And you still have the same friends you've had for years — good people I might add. You even stopped seeing Jared because you didn't think it was fair to lead him on." He angled his head. "Inside, you're still the same person you've always been. Good. Honorable."

"But not so good that I'd forgive you."

"So I've noticed." He blew out a breath. "C'mon, let's go save Jared."

We weaved through the crowd, Logan's palm lightly brushing my lower back and sending a tingle up my spine. I considered objecting but didn't want him to think his touch affected me.

"You're back." Jared flashed us a lopsided grin.

Ms. Abs seized the moment and switched her attention to Logan. "I loved Wars and Ruination."

She went on, breaking down the meaning of various scenes but I tuned her out. I hadn't seen the movie or read the book. Or any of Logan's books, for that matter.

Jared nudged me. "Looks like they're hitting it off," he said for my ears only.

Were they? I tuned back in.

"I'd love to hear more about what you're writing now," she said.

"I'm in between projects. There's this manuscript I just finished though. Shelby has it."

My eyes widened. I hadn't read a single page.

"I'm waiting to see what she says before I pass it on to my publisher." He eyed me.

My lips formed an O as I tried to muster up a response.

"I need her blessing since a lot of it's about her." Logan hadn't taken his eyes off me.

No sane woman would pursue Logan after those comments. After Tiffany made it so obvious that her interest was in Logan, Jared probably wouldn't want to be second best. He'd avoid her. Which meant my work there was done.

I raised my cup. "I need a refill." I spun and booked it, determined to avoid all three of them the rest of the night.

Chapter Seven

Monday morning, I started work earlier than usual, opened escrow for Logan and called him with an update. We talked for more than half an hour about what came next, the home inspection process and when escrow would close.

And he didn't once tell me he loved me or try to line up our next meeting. Maybe he had hit it off with Ms. Abs after all. But thoughts like that wouldn't make my day any more pleasant. Unless... maybe if he did take up with her, I'd have the solid proof I needed that Logan was scum. It would get me out of limbo. Yes, that's what I needed.

Tuesday came and went without a word from Logan or Mr. Fellows. The listing agent on Fellows' house called to say they were still considering our request. As near as I could tell, both his and Logan's deal was still on.

Wednesday evening, I went to the gym. After my last lap around the pool, I dried off and dressed then hit the weight room. I sighed at the lack of free machines. Every single one I wanted was already being used.

"I'm almost done here. Just another couple minutes."

Recognizing Logan's voice immediately, I jerked around. Since when did he go to my gym? My eyes swept over him. He looked gorgeous. His sweats were loose but they weren't the thick kind that looked bulky. The only thing bulky about him was his thighs and tight butt. And why didn't guys wear loose shirts to work out? Well, they did but only the ones with weight problems. The guys who had bodies like Logan always showed off their muscles. Muscles... I tried not to picture them flexing as he...

Logan smiled smugly. "If you gawk, I might think you like me."

I closed my mouth and scanned the area for a free machine.

"Have you heard back yet?" Logan exhaled as he gently let the weights descend again.

"No. I'm going to call when I get in the office."

"Any news from the Mr. Fellows camp?"

I shook my head. "No."

"It's all yours. I'll talk to you later." He rose and waved.

I watched him stroll down the carpeted walkway without turning back. Had he lost interest or not? I'd thought he finished with me at the party but his comment about his manuscript had given me the distinct opposite impression. After a very business-like conversation Monday, I'd expected some flirting or something. Nothing.

I adjusted the weight and began my sets while I obsessed on Logan and whether he still intended to chase me. Damn him for drawing me in again.

◆ ◆ ◆

Janice, the receptionist, poked her head in my office. "Line one is for you." By her look of pity, I knew who it was.

I picked up the phone and punched the flashing button. "Hi, Mr. Fellows, I was just about to call you. I, uh... I heard back." I paused but Mr. Fellows wasn't into filler. If conversation stopped, he only added to the dead air with more silence. "They refused your request. Since the appraisal came in well over the selling price, despite the needed repairs, they feel you're still getting a great deal. They're confident if they put the house on the market again, they'll get what they want. I'm afraid I'm going to have to agree with them on that."

"Fair enough. Escrow's still scheduled to close on the fifth?"

"Yes." No argument? Could it be that easy? Maybe I should ask him outright if he wants to cancel escrow. Or maybe I could be more subtle about it. "Today's the last day of the inspection contingency. I'll need you to sign off on it."

"I can stop by around two. Does that suit you?"

My eyes bugged. Was he really going through with it? What the hell changed?

When I hung up, I called Logan, anxious to share the good news about his house. And of course, that damned indifference sucked me in. "We're in escrow," I announced, holding the phone between my shoulder and ear as I scrolled through my email. "Any preference on when we do the inspection?"

"No, I'm flexible. Just set it up and let me know. How's it going with Mr. Fellows?"

That was the second time he'd asked me about the Fellows deal. Why would Logan care? "Great. Looks like his feet warmed up."

"Good to hear."

Yes, it was. But why did Mr. Fellows go from paranoid and over-cautious to Mellow Fellows? He would arrive shortly to sign off on the papers. Once done, it would be quite a trick for him to back out. The deal was as good as closed.

Several minutes later, a huge grin greeted me as I looked up from my computer. My, Mr. Fellows was in a good mood and anxious to sign, judging by how early he was. "Hi. Have a seat." I pushed the ready stack of papers toward him.

"Don't mind if I do." He snatched up the pen and began flipping through the papers, stopping now and then to scribble his signature. "I have a really good feeling about this house."

"Great." But why the one-eighty? "Me, too."

I verified each signature as he passed me the papers, one by one. When he handed me the last document, I slowly exhaled, my shoulders unbunching. I'd done it. My hard work and patience had finally paid off.

"Let's celebrate. Dinner's on me." Mr. Fellows rose and grabbed his jacket off the back of his chair.

"It's only four. A little early for dinner." But my growling stomach disagreed.

"By the time we get there and order, it'll be dinnertime. C'mon. I know a great place. There's someone I want to talk to and he'll be there. I can kill two birds with one stone."

That was Mr. Fellows, efficient business man through and through.

And I liked him. Not only that, but I wanted to celebrate with him. I followed Mr. Fellows in my own car and despite his foot's reluctance to make contact with the accelerator, we arrived before my stomach imploded.

The Boat House. That was his idea of eating well. Not that I minded.

As soon as we sat, Marcia, the same surly dark-haired waitress who'd served Logan and I, stopped by to take our drink order then dashed off.

Mr. Fellows waved to someone behind me. "Oh, great. He's here. I can introduce you."

I swiveled in my chair to see... Logan. A moment later, he stood at our table.

Just great. Hadn't I been exposed to him enough today between the gym and calling him later with the update? Not really. If I were to be honest with myself, I couldn't get enough of him.

"Logan, you know Shelby, realtor extraordinaire."

If Fellows knew I'd met Logan, they must have talked about me. Hm..."Hi," I said.

"Nice to see you again." Logan gave me a polite smile as though I were only his realtor. "This is unexpected."

Was it? Or had he planned it? I couldn't be sure.

"Isn't that something? Small world," Mr. Fellows said. "Logan, why don't you join us?"

Logan looked innocently to me for confirmation. No smoldering looks? No declaring his love? What was he up to? It wasn't as if I could blow him off and appear rude in front of Mr. Fellows. But was there anyone in this town who Logan didn't know? "Uhm, yeah, have a seat." I scooted over to make room.

"I'd love to," he said pleasantly then embarked on conversations with Mr. Fellows that were so far out of my sphere of interest, all I could do was nod now and then. To my surprise, Logan knew an awful lot about sailing and cars.

Our food arrived and they moved on to sports which wasn't any better for me. I laughed at the appropriate times and enjoyed the great food.

When we were ready to leave, Mr. Fellows grabbed the check. Logan reached into his wallet but Mr. Fellows held up a hand. "It's on me. It's the least I can do for all your help."

What help?

"It was no trouble," Logan said.

"There I was, lost in my own little real estate hell when this young man pulled me out," Mr. Fellows told me. "How'd you learn so much about real estate, Logan?"

Since when did my ex, the famous writer, become an expert on buying and selling? If he'd known that much about the industry, he wouldn't have been asking so many questions over the last couple days.

Logan grinned at me then back to Mr. Fellows. "I'm a good listener."

So he'd taken everything I said and repeated it to Mr. Fellows who wouldn't listen to me but he'd listened to a celebrity. Did Logan seek Mr. Fellows out on my behalf or was he in the right place at the right time? Either way, Logan saved my ass. But did he help out just to get me in his bed or did he really love me? I wasn't so sure anymore.

"Well, thank you for dinner." I rose and collected my purse.

"You're quite welcome. We'll talk soon."

"I'll walk you to your car," Logan said, his hand finding its way to my lower back to guide me.

I nodded and headed to my Lexus, stopping at the driver's side.

"Goodnight," he said, turning to leave.

"Wait." I grabbed his solid upper arm and he froze. Stretching up on my toes, I brushed his cheek with my lips and lowered again. "Thank you."

His eyes locked onto mine and narrowed. "For what?"

"It's obvious you talked to him. That was nice of you."

He shrugged and continued watching me. Would he kiss me? I wanted him to. No, I didn't. That would only complicate my life and nothing had changed between us. Nothing majorly important anyway. But would he try? My breathing slowed as I waited.

"I'd kiss you right now," he said softly, tracing his fingertips down my cheek. "But you're not ready yet."

I watched him walk away, knowing I wouldn't sleep much that night. Thoughts of him would consume me. As if he didn't already own me, body and soul.

"I love you, Shelby."

Yes, he did. Everything in me believed it wholeheartedly. Ours was the rare and special love that would last forever.

"I love you, too." I gulped in a lungful of air and the delicious ache laced through me. No man had ever touched me like that. No other man ever would.

"Shelby," he whispered in my ear. "Let it go, baby."

The little tickle built until my body quivered and I moaned.

I gasped, opening my eyes as the last of the quivers subsided and I curled into my comforter.

Oh, Lord, I'd just had a wet dream about Logan. And it had been good. No, it had been great. Not only that, I'd just had a killer orgasm without having to compromise my principles or put myself in a position where he could dump me.

Life was good.

I didn't mind that the sun wasn't up and I still had an hour before my alarm would go off. The lost hour of sleep had been a fair trade-off for the pleasant surprise upon waking. I sprung out of bed and threw my work-out clothes on, in a hurry to make it to the gym before it got crowded. When I arrived, the parking lot was nearly empty.

Inside, I reveled at all the machines available to me, nearly giddy with excitement.

By the time I'd finished with my weights routine, the space had filled with people and clanging metal as the various machines worked.

"Good morning."

Logan. Everywhere I went, there he was. Today though, the irritation didn't stab at me. In fact, I was glad to see him. He was wearing me down, turning me into putty.

"Morning," I returned.

"You saved me a phone call. I was going to confirm the inspection today."

"Right." I smiled. Yep, the last of my resistance was failing. "It's scheduled for noon."

"See you at noon then." He strolled off and began his workout.

I did a few laps around the pool then grabbed my things and headed for my car to go home for a shower. Logan met me at the Lexus as if he'd been waiting for me.

"Hey, what's up?" I threw my bag on the passenger side seat.

"Just wondering what you're doing later, after the inspection."

I frowned, the muscles in my entire body tensing as though I was still using the weight machine. "Probably going back to work and reading the inspection report." I wouldn't ask why he wanted to know. It could lead to me agreeing to a date.

"Thought you might want to get together later. Have a drink?"

He'd softened me up but it had to stop. After all, none of his actions were solid proof he loved me. And even though I knew I'd never get a guarantee that he'd love me forever, I needed at least the hope of it.

I sighed, vowing to resist. "No, Logan. You and me, it's not going to work. We need to keep our relationship strictly business. I'm sorry."

Logan's face fell, reminding me of the boy I knew long ago. "Why won't it work? I know you still love me."

"How would you know that? Did I say that? No, I didn't. So why would you believe it?"

"Like you said, saying I love you doesn't mean much. It's what you do. Like ending things with Jared, protesting too much when I talk about your feelings for me... following my career."

Ginny! I'd beat her to a pulp. No, not really but she'd get some stern words. "I have to go. Can we do this another time? Like, never." I moved to get inside my car and his arm blocked me. I spun and glared. "Please get out of my way."

"You're still mad. I get it. And I can't really blame you. But, geez, Shelby, what's a guy gotta do to make it right?"

"Nothing. You can't make it right. You can't fix it with the fat commission on the house or tempt me by taking away my troubles with Mr. Fellows. You can't buy me, Logan."

Logan's eyes narrowed. "Buy you? Is that what you think I'm doing?" He scoffed. "Because if I wanted to buy a woman, I could do it a lot cheaper than dropping over a million in cash on a house." His jaw ticked. I'd pissed him off. Good.

I slammed my car door shut, stretched up to my full five seven and lifted my chin. "Why me, Logan? What about me makes you try so hard? Is it because I keep saying no? You like your women to play hard to get?"

"I like you, however I can get you. Just you."

Oh, wow. The way he said it in that low growl made my bones melt. But I couldn't let him get to me. Shaking my head, I sighed.

"You've got a rockin' body but your nose is a little too long and your lips are too full. And I like my women blonde and without the attitude. And if you were an actress, they'd tell you to get a boob job."

"What?" I shook my head. This was not the way to woo me.

"And yet you're perfect to me. Damn it, Shelby." He pushed me, slamming his hands against my car on either side of me. "I've never met anyone more beautiful or anyone I wanted more than you."

I blinked.

"I was scared. When I came here, it was with the sole purpose of fixing things with you. It was hopeless, of course, but I had to do it anyway. Your attitude since I've come back has made me wonder if it really is hopeless. After the conversation with Jared, I knew it wasn't. Even if this is all pointless, I'd still rather grow old here and see you once in a while than live the rest of my life without you in it."

His words sent a shudder through my veins, renewed love into my heart and air whooshed into my lungs, bringing hope with it. But unlike Logan, I couldn't afford even the tiniest sliver of hope. It's what hurls you into the living but once taken away, shatters your life.

"The idea behind the house wasn't so you could get a commission. The house is for us, to raise our children. That's why I wanted to make sure you loved it. I want to create a life with you. I want forever with you. I knew when I came back that you might not want the same thing but I had to at least put it out there. If I did nothing, like the last nine years, that would only ensure I'd never get you back."

Logan had no idea what he was saying, had no concept of what forever really meant. Maybe something happened in Hollywood and he'd had a wild urge to run for safety. Me. I was safe.

I gently moved his arms so I wasn't imprisoned and took a deep breath. "The thing is, Logan, it makes no difference if I want those things with you or not. Because

I already know I can never have them. It doesn't matter what you say or what you do, because I'll never be able to trust you. I can never give you my whole heart. We can't have a forever without that."

He nodded slowly. "I understand. But as a writer, I can work from anywhere. I'll just wait right here until you can trust me again. As long as it takes." He opened my car door.

I hesitated, watching him, then turned and got in front of the wheel. He gently closed the door and walked away.

My body fused with the car seat as all my zest for life left with Logan. I sat there in the gym parking lot, unmoving except for my trembling hands.

Chapter Eight

At noon on the dot, Logan pulled up in his Jaguar in front of his future house. I waited as he got out and closed the distance, feeling extremely awkward after our last words. A part of me felt bad but the other part of me knew that Logan would get over it. His love wasn't real. If it was something close to love, it wouldn't last anyway. Just like before. Mine on the other hand...

"Hey." He shoved his hands in his pocket.

I nodded toward the approaching truck. "That's Rafe, our inspector. While he's doing his job, you and I will do our own inspection, you know, check out the house more thoroughly, case the neighborhood and that sort of thing."

Rafe sidled up and I introduced them. I let us into the house and he got to work.

"Now's the time to make sure you really want it, see if it meets your needs," I said.

He grinned. "Only if you'll do the same."

Butterflies rioted in my stomach at the thought of being with Logan in that way, sharing a life with him. "I have my own house, Logan. I'm not moving in with you. We're not going to live happily ever after here."

"You can keep the other house. Rent it out." He opened a hallway closet. "Lots of storage space."

I ignored his comment, but inside I longed to make his fantasy my own.

Logan and I went our separate ways, me searching for anything that might decrease the value and Logan making double sure that the house would provide for all his needs.

He found me later in the kitchen pantry. "So what do you say we have dinner after this and we can look at the report together?"

"It's as if this morning's chat never happened." I frowned. "Look, Logan, whatever you think you feel for me, you'll get over it."

"I disagree. If I haven't gotten over it in nine years, I never will. Believe me, I tried."

I pushed past him and out of the pantry then glanced around for the inspector, wishing the house wasn't vacant. Occupants would have given me a buffer.

"He's on the roof. Can't hear us. There's no one to save you now." Logan grinned.

"Let's just say I believed you and we fell into bed. It might last a while and we'd probably have a great ride. But I'd always be wondering when you were going to leave. There would always be a part of me watching to see if you're looking at other girls."

He leaned against the granite counter. "I don't want anyone but you. You have it in your head that I'm fickle and unpredictable. But it was never a matter of not loving you anymore or leaving you for someone else. I never stopped loving you in the first place, Shelby."

"So you keep saying." My resistance was dissolving and my body hummed for wanting him. I needed distance. When he turned around, I darted down the hallway and slipped into the master bedroom. A moment later, I heard the door close. He'd followed me.

"Depriving yourself of me won't make you love me less."

I spun around to see him leaning against the door, blocking my exit. "Can we just drop it, Logan?"

"That's not what you want. You don't want me to leave again."

I folded my arms over my chest, brows raised.

"I was just a boy trying to find my way. It was hard enough being several hundred miles from you and never knowing what you're really thinking. Even before that, I always felt I wasn't good enough for you. You were... everything I wanted, everything I knew I couldn't hold onto. And it was painful, almost unbearable being with you and yet not being with you. So I broke up with you, hoping it would be easier. It wasn't. And every day since then, I've thought about you, wishing I could do it all over again. The reason I got photographed with so many girls was because I kept trying to get over you. But in the end, none of them were you. And, finally, I got tired of hearing myself whine."

The way he told it, his life mirrored mine. I shivered and turned to look out the window. "Doesn't change anything, Logan. I'd still be wondering when you were going to get scared and run again. Even if we were together, there would be nothing to hold you here. Like you said, you can write from anywhere."

"Shelby?" The door opened. "There you are," Rafe said. "Been looking all over for you guys."

Rafe debriefed us, got a check from Logan and shook his hand. I walked them out and locked the door behind me. I did not want to get trapped in there with Logan again. My car was just a few yards away. Freedom.

I waved at Rafe as he drove off and when I turned to my car, Logan was leaning against the door. I steeled myself for more, knowing I couldn't hold out much longer. My throat ached from unshed tears and my hands trembled.

"I won't keep you," he said. "I just want to say one thing..."

"Which is?"

"I'm not going anywhere. I love you, Shelby. Always have." His eyes grew shiny and he pushed himself off my car, strolling to his own. "Read the damn manuscript," he threw over his shoulder.

Logan had really gotten to me this time. Not his words. What devastated me was his intensity and sincerity, and the last moment when his eyes glistened. Emotion. Possibly love. And for that instant, I truly believed him—just like I had years ago. My tendency to fall too hard for him terrified me. What if I gave in and opened myself up only to have him discard me again like leftovers? The very thought knotted my insides and moistened my palms.

In a daze, I drove home, knowing I wouldn't accomplish a damn thing at work. Flying through the door of my house, I tossed my purse on the couch and retrieved the manuscript from underneath the couch. The first few chapters described me, our relationship, his relocation to Los Angeles and how much he wished he lived in Sacramento, with me.

My first spring without Shelby, my dad went in for a routine doctor's appointment. His only complaint had been that his lower energy level. Since he was in his forties, he wasn't worried. After more several more appointments and endless tests, his diagnosis of bladder cancer came as a shock. He hated being thought of as weak and he couldn't handle being pitied, so he made me promise not to tell anyone. For him, it was about pride.

All I could do was hope Dad got better soon. Between school and homework, I helped him through chemo and happily served as his caretaker. Because I lay awake each night worrying about him, I spent most of my days sleep deprived and exhausted. When I spoke with Shelby, I would stood outside and talked so I wouldn't disturb my dad. Some days, I couldn't return Shelby's calls at all. Any extra activity became a choice between that or my dad. Every day was filled with stress that I would fall behind on my studies, so Shelby took a backseat. And I couldn't even tell her why.

I wanted to tell Shelby about my dad, and how many

times I thought of her while I waited for him during his doctor visits. But I couldn't break the vow of silence I'd made with my dad.

And I didn't want her to worry. Mostly, I didn't want her to know how difficult my life had become. She would only feel bad and I couldn't burden her that way.

After his surgery, the doctors said there would be a long convalescence and likely more chemo up the road to make sure all the cancer was gone. I didn't want to watch my dad go through all that pain. But I did. And at the same time, I cleaned the house, shopped for groceries, and took care of him while keeping up pretenses with Shelby.

I had made friends with a girl who lived a couple houses away. She'd seen my dad outside when we left for the hospital one day and figured out he wasn't well. Since I didn't have to keep secrets from her, I could open up and be myself. On the rare occasion that I had downtime, she and I would sit out front on the porch steps and just talk.

One Saturday while my dad was napping, we sat on the steps. When our conversation lulled, her hand slowly slid over mine. I didn't resist and before I realized what she was going to do, she kissed me. She could never be Shelby but that didn't matter. I kissed her back. Guilt consumed me for letting my guard down and cheating on Shelby, the girl of my dreams. I hated myself for that.

The next day I broke up with Shelby. Not because I didn't love her but because I wanted to share everything with her and couldn't. I wanted her with me. I'd turned eighteen months before and could leave any time. I wanted to move back home, but with my dad still sick, leaving wasn't an option. Shelby and I needed a clean break so we could both move on.

I cried most of the first day after breaking up with her. I missed her so much, my insides ached. Every time I remembered that I wouldn't be seeing her again, I wanted to curl up into a ball. I told myself that I'd get over her and eventually she'd be only a faded memory.

Knowing that the pain would eventually pass helped me get through the next few months with my dad.

Tears stung my eyes. If only Logan had told me all that. I'd recently seen his father in a photograph with Logan so I knew he was still alive.

I read on.

When my dad was well enough to be on his own, I visited my mom during school vacations, but never with the intention of looking up Shelby. Even though it had been months since I'd broken up with her, my emotions were still too raw. Shelby didn't know I had let another girl kiss me while we were still together. But I knew.

And I was a coward. If I didn't put myself out there, she couldn't say no. If she never rejected me, I would always have hope.

Seventeen months since I'd last seen Shelby, I still couldn't forget her. Yielding to my longing, I took a road trip from Los Angeles to Sacramento, vowing to win Shelby back. The drive was long and tedious but thoughts of Shelby and I renewing our love spurred me on. I couldn't wait to see her.

My mom's house was warm and inviting and my room was exactly the same, as if waiting for my return. But I couldn't stay. I thought of nothing but reuniting with Shelby. I planned to explain everything and she'd welcome me back. Continuing a long distance relationship was out of the question, of course. I'd move back for her, just as we'd originally planned.

I didn't want to call her, preferring to surprise her in person. I imagined how happy she'd be to see me. It didn't take long to squash that dream. I'd been in front of her house working up the nerve to knock on the door when a guy about our age waltzed up to her front porch and beat me to it. Shelby came out, kissed him on the cheek, ducked back inside to grab something then strolled with him to his car, hand in hand.

She'd moved on.

Broken hearted, I returned to Los Angeles. After that, I occasionally visited my mom and sister, but I never tried to look Shelby up again.

The next section detailed his first manuscript, his journey to publication and his first movie deal, the production and the premier. He told of the excitement and his first multi-book deal and the thrill when his books hit the best seller lists.

I was at the top of my field, the envy of other writers, with no shortage of women. But something was missing. I wanted someone by my side who'd always be there. And all I could think about was Shelby. After all this time, I still loved her. When I thought of the woman I wanted to grow old with, have children with, it was always Shelby. It wasn't possible, of course. The three years I'd dated Shelby and she'd never once told me she loved me.

I squeezed my eyes shut. He was right. I'd never told him, even after we'd made love. I'd been afraid that once I said those words, it would all disappear. It was no wonder his fears and insecurities triumphed.

My heart pounded in my chest and I turned to the next page.

But we'd been together nearly three years. Shelby had to have loved me, whether she'd verbalized it or not. If she did once, she could again. I called my sister in Sacramento to see if she could find out anything about her. For all I knew, she'd married and already had four children.

Within a few days, my sister called to give me the news. Shelby was still single and, according to a friend of a friend, dated occasionally. Her relationships never lasted longer than a few months though. She was a successful real estate agent who, in her spare time, obsessed with health and fitness.

All signs pointed to someone who didn't stay in a relationship because they were still hung up on someone else and who worked off her tension for the same reason. It was a thin hope, but it was hope.

I contacted my real estate agent in Los Angeles to put my house up for sale, and began arrangements to relocate.

For the first time in nine years, I had real hope, a purpose. And now, I embark on my journey. To Shelby. And if she no longer wants me, I'll wait until she loves me again. As long as it takes.

All that time, he really did love me. I could blow the entire book off as a scheme to con me. But it wasn't. Deep in my soul, I knew Logan. The boy I remembered didn't have a con of this magnitude in him.

And the man he'd become had grown into a man I could love forever — would love forever.

I wiped my eyes and checked my watch. It was after eleven and I'd been reading for hours. Would he still be up? Did I care? No, I didn't. Grabbing my keys, I tore out of the house and jumped into my car. The few miles to his house were excruciatingly painful. With my bad luck in love, he had probably already come to his senses and concluded I was a cruel bitch only out to torture him. Who could blame him?

Pulling up to the curb at his house, I snagged a tissue from the glove box, wiped the tears from my cheeks and flew out of the car. I raced up the walkway and pounded on the door, my breath coming in pants.

His door swung open. My chin quivered and my eyes pooled. Immediately attentive, he stepped over the threshold and grasped my shoulders. "Shelby, what's wrong?"

"You were right," I sobbed. "I love you. I never stopped loving you. And I should have told you back then."

Logan grinned. "It's about time." The next instant, I was in his arms, his hands stroking my hair.

I bawled, drenching his t-shirt. I felt like a fool letting it all out on his front porch for all the world to see. But I was beyond caring. I was tired of denial. At that point, even if he changed his mind and dumped me, in a way I'd be free. But something told me he wouldn't.

He hugged me tighter and eventually my crying turned into a soft sigh. "Better now?"

"Yes." Much better—now that he was holding me. I'd have to thank Ginny. Later though. I had something to do first — namely, Logan. I lifted my head from his chest. "Can you forgive me for not telling you back then?"

Logan brushed my hair off my face and met my eyes. "We'll trade. You have to forgive me for being a coward for the nine longest years of my life."

"I can do that." I smiled through the new tears.

He cupped my face and lowered his mouth to mine. His gentle kiss ended all too quickly, leaving me shivering. Then he scooped me up and carried me inside.

I needed to say it again, to make sure he knew. "I love you, Logan."

"I know. And this time, it's forever," he whispered.

The End

About Veronica Blade

Veronica Blade resides in northern Nevada with her husband and furbabies. By day she runs the family business, but each night she slips away to spin her tales. She writes stories about falling in love and lives vicariously through her characters. Except her heroes and heroines lead far more interesting lives—and they are always way hotter.

You can visit Veronica Blade on Facebook, check out her website at VeronicaBlade.com or follow her on Twitter @VeronicaBlade. You can even e-mail her at veronica@ veronicablade.com. She loves hearing from readers!

Please turn the page for sneak peeks of other books by Veronica Blade.

More Titles by Veronica Blade

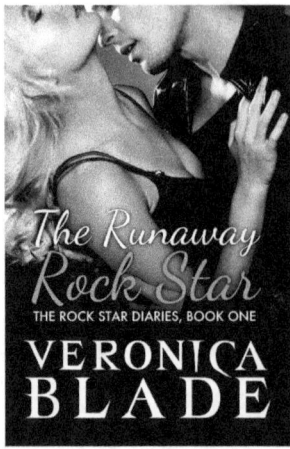

An infamous bad-boy rocker falls for a small-town girl who has no idea who he is. Considering his reputation, that's probably a good thing.

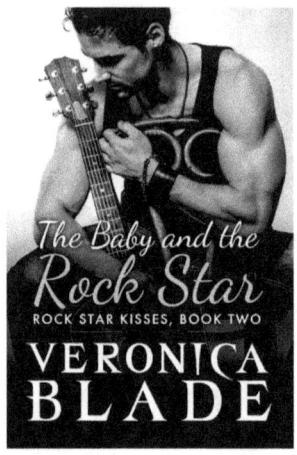

He's working hard to get his life back on track after three years of alcohol-induced oblivion. She can't forget their one wild night together—that he doesn't remember.

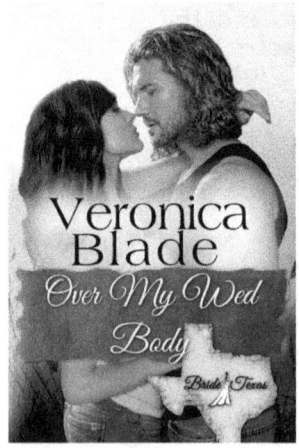

When Hunter realizes he botched the annulment of his marriage to his longtime friend, he must decide if she and their marriage are worth fighting for.

A micro trilogy including Single-Handed, Singled Out (book two) & Single-minded (book three).

More Titles by Veronica Blade

When good-girl Maddie switches places with her famous bad-girl twin Jackie, she has some pretty high stilettos to fill.

A Cinderella who spends her nights as a wolf. A prince with a taste for blood.

SHAPES OF AUTUMN SERIES

Thrown to the Wolves: The Legend of Hannah & Eli (prequel)

My Wolf's Bane (book one)

Wolves at the Door (book two)

Dead Wolf Walking (book three)

The Dark Wolf (book four)

Lord of the Wolves (book five)

Different species. Mortal enemies. It'll never work, but they'll die trying.

A newbie witch enlists help from the scrumptious school bad-boy to make her life and death choice between two battling covens.

The witch queen must make the impossible choice between abandoning the throne and her people, or spending eternity without the man she loves.

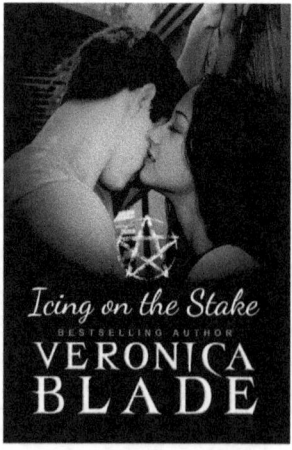

Sofia lays her hard-won anonymity on the line by saving the most popular boy in school. Worse, she's been exposed to the vampire hunters who attacked him.

For updates on releases,

please visit
VeronicaBlade.com

Acknowledgements

I had such a great time writing this story for the anthology Set Up for Love with Virna and Susan Hatler. I am so grateful to them for: (1) inviting me into the project; (2) babying me along the way; (3) picking up my slack; and (4) just being awesome in general.

Virna and Susan were sweeter and more pleasant to work with than I could have hoped for and I feel very fortunate to have been able to work with them. I'm honored that they had the faith in me to pull off my end of it.

Biggest thanks to my dear hubby for putting up with the neglect whenever I'm writing (which is the majority of the time) and his unwavering support throughout my writing career. I couldn't ask for a better man to share my life with.

Veronica Blade

www.ingramcontent.com/pod-product-compliance
Lightning Source LLC
Chambersburg PA
CBHW070456130626
46555CB00003B/1022